# THE LIGHT YOU SEEK

*CASSANDRA*

Katy Tackes

THE LIGHT YOU SEEK ~ CASSANDRA
Katy Tackes
Copyright © 2023 by Katy Tackes
Published by inSpīrus8™

inSpīrus8™ Publishing
inspire.us.8@gmail.com

Cover art: The Light You Seek, by Katy Tackes, Visit the art gallery: www.KatyTackesART.com

The Light You Seek ~ Cassandra / Katy Tackes. -- 1st ed.
ISBN: 978-0-9904572-4-4 (print)

Prologue

Ancient Days

For some these pages will bleed the Truth, for others they will just bleed…

The year was one I could not tell; not because I had been sworn to secrecy, but some things were kept buried…out of reach. Just imagine a time when water turned to wine and mystic tales were spun on the wind, though never committed to ink and spine.

Somewhere in the vastness of the Persian Empire, a cloud of darkness approached. This ground swell of doom arose with the western wind, and brought chaos along with it. It was a time of destruction for the empire, and upheaval of its social order. These conquerors held worldly gain and supremacy above All.  Their cunning annihilation of ancient wisdom was their first execution.

This insatiable power drove the most pious of families into exile.  The initiated, who carefully guarded the fragments of luminous wisdom entrusted to them, rode away on the desert wind.  Deep into hiding they went; behind great walls of sand and stone, into the darkest of caverns.  With them, followed the noble traditions and practices which ensured humanity's enlightenment and evolution…up until now.

# Chapter One

Some eighteen years ago, Yazd, Iran

Stillness loomed upon the remote desert location during that mid-September night. Deep into the evening hour, the crescent moon cast its silvery veil, cloaking the defunct Tower of Silence, as it stood witness at the edge of town. The ancient village was a mosaic of adobe architecture that glowed with golden-hued light against the midnight blue sky.

Under the shadow of an 800-year-old mosque, lay the rubble of the once illustrious throne. The broken dwelling of the Magi had been abandoned, save one soul--Sephira, the radiant. She was the keeper of the flame, and last of the royal bloodline.

The religious order that claimed the land for itself tolerated one remnant of the old tradition of fire; they allowed Sephira to maintain the sacred flame, as long as she kept the ancient ways to herself. But there was one secret she could no longer keep inside…

"Just one more push!" The command came in Farsi from Hasood, the haggard old woman, who mysteriously appeared at the gate of the walled home just a few months ago. Hasood had injected herself into the young woman's life upon discovering Sephira was alone, unwed, and with child. She portrayed herself to be hungry and forlorn; then offered midwifing skills, in trade for food and shelter. Sephira's kind heart welcomed Hasood; she appreciated the much-needed support Hasood lent during her concealed pregnancy.

The agony of labor intensified. Sephira's delicate hands clenched the mattress as waves of pain overtook her being. Her body contorted with each excruciating contraction, but she refused to make a sound in fear of being discovered. She had managed to stay obscured during these last few months of pregnancy, while Hasood tended to the daily chores. The old one, handled all that took place beyond the high walls of the courtyard under the watchful eyes of the powerful Imam.

Hasood sat upon an iron stool at the foot of the bed, where the expectant mother coiled in pain. She rocked back and forth on the three-legged seat; pulling at Sephira's ankles as she heartlessly demanded once again, "Push--give me everything you have--push!"

Her voice was harsh and so were her motions as she manipulated the delivery. With one final thrust, the baby plunged into Hasood's hands, where she deftly tied off the umbilical cord. Then, reaching into the pocket of her stained skirt, she retrieved a rusty, dual-edged dagger, and used it to callously sever the baby from its mother. She probed into the baby's airway with her crooked finger, then turned it upside down and landed a fierce slap upon its backside.

The baby's sudden gasp for air, was followed by wailing, deep from within the innocent one's soul.

Hasood hastily wiped the baby down, and laid the infant on the few rags she had spread out earlier. She swaddled it tightly, attempting to silence the powerful crying.

"She is strong-willed, a force to be reckoned with, based on the fire within her," Hasood said with disdain. She shoved the swaddled bundle into the crux of her left arm, and quickly began gathering her belongings with her free hand.

Feeble from the many hours of labor, Sephira summoned her strength enough to whisper, "A baby girl…the Light of my light." She smiled, as tears of joy escaped her weary eyes.

"Please bring her to me, Hasood. Let me hold my precious girl." She reached out toward the old woman, in order to receive the newborn.

By now, Hasood had made her way to the door, where she paused and turned toward Sephira. She watched, with a grin on her face, as confusion unraveled around the new mother.

Sephira made another desperate plea to hold her baby.

Hasood placed the crying infant into a basket, near the doorway, and slowly walked back to the foot of the bed.

"Shh, shh, shh...you are losing a lot of blood," her tone was slow, indifferent, and disturbingly calm. Hasood leaned over Sephira's quivering body, as she cunningly swayed her head from side to side in feigned concern. Her rough hand slithered up the inside of Sephira's right leg and paused at the birthmark upon her upper thigh. It designated the lineage of a true and noble bloodline--one more ancient than those who grasp at the kingdom today.

"The royal *stain*," Hasood whispered to herself as she indignantly smeared blood, from the birth, over Sephira's rightful mark. Hasood's lips tightened with repugnance, as she poisoned the air with her voice once again, "If someone does not help you soon, you will not last more than a few moments."

She proceeded to cover Sephira's nose and mouth with one hand, while grabbing the dagger with the other. Her wretched fingers were swift. In one foul motion, she sliced deep into Sephira's femoral artery, and stood back to watch the life blood escape her beautiful body.

Hasood moved to the foot of the bed, where she wiped the dagger on the bedsheets. She slowly stepped away from the growing pool of blood, until she had backed herself up against the door.

"The flame is now in my hands. I control the fate of the Kingdom!" she proclaimed, grabbing the basket, and running out through the back door. The door slammed shut behind her, as a rush of air extinguished Sephira's flame.

Upon reaching the outer gate of the walled courtyard, Hasood was met by the pounding thrust of sand and air against her entire body. The pelting sand pierced her cheeks and hands like the points of a thousand daggers. The air pulsated around her in a powerful and rhythmic force, yet it was barely audible. Hasood looked up, into the sky, where she saw the metal blades of a black whirling bird stealthily cut across the crescent moon. She tightened her grip on the basket as she turned to run away. But she had no chance; the karmic winds were swift that night. Hasood was stopped—dead—in her tracks.

Chapter Two


Present day, Vienna, Virginia


Sadie Jones exited the corner onto Church Street when she heard the blistering speed of drumming blasting from the open doors of the Vienna Vinyl Exchange. Classic Led Zeppelin, "Dazed and Confused" was lamenting the blues from half-way up the block. Visiting The Exchange had become her weekly ritual; a welcomed escape from the years of being home schooled by her father.

As Sadie entered through the doors, she saw Jason, the clerk behind the counter. Her pace slowed as she walked closer to him, taking in the view. Jason was ruggedly handsome, with waves of blonde hair, that Sadie let her fingers surf through, in her imagination. He had cool, blue eyes and a perfectly chiseled body that could melt hearts all over Virginia. But this guy was off the market, or rather, he was captivated, by his dreams of dating Sadie…one day.

Sadie watched Jason. His eyes were closed and his motions were exaggerated as he frantically drummed the air to the beat of the music with a set of sticks, he kept in his back pocket. It wasn't until the final strike of the imaginary cymbal that he opened his eyes and caught a glimpse of her presence.

He stopped abruptly, embarrassed as hell, yet not willing to lose the opportunity to speak with her. He called out, "Hey! Hi, Sadie," an uncharacteristic crack in his voice betrayed his manhood. He cleared his throat with a cough then piped up again, "It's really great to see you, Sadie. Are you looking for anything in particular today? Or, uh…are you here to see me?" He cringed at his own lame attempt at flirting, while secretly hoping for a hint at the latter.

Sadie lifted her gaze, and playfully batted her long, dark lashes toward Jason, then called back, "You know I'm here for you Jason, it's always about you baby!" She smiled and winked at him before she headed to the back wall, where her favorite selections could be found.

Jason pocketed his sticks and pretended to work, while his sight wrapped around his favorite girl. Sadie sure was a beauty. Not just a 'head-turner' beautiful; she had that mythic beauty; the kind poets wrote about and sculptors dreamt about just before they breathed life into their creation. What made her even more alluring, was she had no idea of the power her beauty held.

Her burst of chestnut-brown curls was usually restrained by a colorful tie-died scarf that inevitably set one or two locks free, framing her striking features. She rarely wore make-up; she didn't need it. Her sensuous figure flawlessly displayed her '60's flower-child rags she picked up from various vintage stores she often frequented.

Jason watched as she glided across the floor.

Her long, emerald-green dress teased him with momentary glimpses of her statuesque legs as she made her way down the aisle. She stopped at her regular spot and tilted her head to one side while she slowly thumbed through the bin of old classics.

His vision traced the length of her neck. He imagined himself alongside her; close enough to sense her heartbeat pulsing from her softly perfumed skin.

Suddenly, his clandestine view was interrupted, by the sirens of a passing fire truck. A second truck approached and ripped by, then the paramedics rounded the corner. The engines streaked by the store front with lights flashing and sirens wailing.

"What the heck is going on out there?" Sadie murmured under her breath. She was distracted, yet she continued leafing through the stack of albums.

The third fire truck sped by the shop with its horns blasting, as if demanding everyone's attention; calling them outside to see what the uproar was about.

"It's close, really close!" Jason warned as he jumped over the counter and went outside to watch the commotion unfold nearby. Everyone from the shop followed him out. Sadie was the last one to the edge of the curb; almost hesitant to view the scene.

The smell of burning wood and plastic began to fill the air as thick, black, smoke rose from the next block over. People from the surrounding shops spilled onto the sidewalk to witness the growing demon-plume obscure the light of the sun. Jason looked past the crowd toward Sadie to make sure she was safe and within his sight.

Sadie was standing on the edge of the sidewalk, stunned by the size and proximity of the fire. She began to back away from the scene until she was pressed up against the bricks of the record shop. Fear began to quell up from the pit of her stomach. Her senses heightened with the roar of the fire.

"Run!" She heard a frantic whisper; it repeated, "Run!" She turned to see who said it, but only the bricks of the wall stood behind her. Frightened and confused, she began to walk away slowly; moving along the wall, almost hugging it, as she reached the entrance of the record shop. Through the doors she could hear Zeppelin's next song, "When the Levee Breaks" reverberating against the glass. She tuned in to the familiar beat in hopes of drowning out the voice calling out to her, but it was no use. "Run! Run!!" she heard it again as she instinctively took a few steps forward. She hesitated at the street corner, but then she took off running, fast--faster as she saw the massive inferno and where the fire trucks had converged.

The flames were leaping into the air, licking, and teasing the electrical wires high above. The fire was fast and hot as it continued to burn out of control. Its appetite was ravenous.

It engulfed and consumed the home; belching up billows of smoke and ash.

Sadie looked up in horror as she pushed her way through the mass of spectators; forcing herself through the crowd. She was struggling to get up front; she was fighting to get home!

Just as she was about to break through the police barricade, surrounding the fiery scene, she was snatched up by her upper arms and yanked away, backwards. Two men restrained her while rushing her into the back seat of a black Crown Vic with dark tinted windows. The sedan had been waiting alongside the curb with its engine running. Before she could scream for help, she was thrust into the car. The doors locked, as it swiftly pulled away—unnoticed—amidst the chaos of the smoke and flames.

"What are you doing?! That's my house! My dad is in there, you asshole, let me go! Let me go!!" she screamed, but no one would listen. Sadie struggled frantically to free herself from their grip, but it tightened around her body. She continued the fight—kicking, screaming, and scratching, at the hands of these brutes to release their hold.

It took a while before her violent thrashing was subdued, mostly by her own exhaustion. She was wheezing for air. Defeat set in once she realized her tears were all she had managed to set free. Breathless, Sadie collapsed back into the seat, conceding, momentarily.

The car entered the expressway and gained speed while swerving through traffic as it repeatedly changed lanes. Sadie could feel her heart beating through her chest. Her bloodshot eyes darted around, attempting to understand the fractured events of the past few minutes, as anger and fear battled for her attention.

Once at full speed, the passenger in the front turned to face Sadie. He reached behind the seat with his large, hairy hand and grabbed Sadie's face by her chin. When she jerked herself away from his unwelcome touch, their eyes met.

The man's face was sallow and his skin was pitted with the scars of childhood chicken pox. He methodically fingered the thick, dark, unruly beard covering his narrow jawline. He sat head and shoulders above the seatback, and from this twisted position his eyes appeared black as coal and were deeply sunken to produce his menacing stare.

His focus latched onto Sadie. He began at her feet then he slowly lifted his lecherous gaze along her entire body; lingering far too long on her bare legs that had become exposed by her fruitless struggle. He caught himself in his disobedient act and reluctantly turned away. After an odd pause, he twisted around again, reaching back for the slit in Sadie's dress. Slowly he lifted the emerald silk with his middle and index fingers, exposing more to his view before covering her legs with the skimpy fabric.

He snarled out orders in a foreign language to the two thugs on either side of her. His breath was rancid and his teeth were stained and crooked. As he turned to face forward again, he deliberately slid his two fingers down and across his nose and mouth, as if tasting Sadie's scent.

She recoiled; frightened and disgusted at the same time. She could still feel the sensation of the back of his intrusive hand rubbing along her bare thigh. Her whole body rejected his presence in a sudden and repulsive withdrawal.

The vile one spewed out more foreign commands, this time to the driver. All Sadie could make out from between his words were, "G7...security...and Dulles".

"Miss Jones!" the man on her left shook her hard to capture her attention. "We are with the Secret Service. We are here to protect you. You must trust us." He pushed her firmly against the seatback. "You have been removed from the scene for your own protection. We are here to take you to safety."

Sadie winced under his tight grip; she could feel his firearm grind deep into her ribcage. Fear provoked her tears once again as her emotions were cornered in, along with her freedom. She pleaded, "Please, let me go! Take me home; that's *my* house that is on fire. I must know if my father is safe, if he got out; is he alright!?" Frustration came to a head as she yelled, "Don't you understand?! Jeezus just turn this beast around and take me home!"

She attempted to wrestle out of their hold once more. But these men had been assigned a mission and they were trained to complete it.

As Sadie turned to make another plea, she felt a cloth cover her nose and mouth just before all light plunged into darkness.

Chapter Three

Green...Black...Green...Black...Green...It took a few seconds before Sadie realized the color show was caused by the blinking of her own eyes, as she awakened from the drug-induced sleep. Her neck was stiff from suspending her head, from her motionless body, for the past half-hour. In her slouched position, all she could make out was the fabric of her green dress. It was crumpled beneath the seatbelt that was cinched tightly across her lap. She clumsily tried to stand up; neglecting the purpose of the seatbelt altogether; she didn't get very far. Her motions were slow and lumbered as she began to struggle with the buckle like a sloppy drunk.

Defiantly, she willed her eyelids to stay open, as she assessed her surroundings. Sunlight beamed in through a few circular windows next to her. The light was persistent in arousing her senses to her current predicament. "Wake up, open your eyes!" she heard echoing in her own mind.

As Sadie emerged from her intoxication, she saw a tall, slender woman approaching down what she slowly recognized to be the aisle of a jet. Once close enough, the winged logo pinned to the woman's navy-blue lapel flickered in the sunlight. The flight attendant leaned over Sadie, into the light, and whispered "My name is Faith; I'll be assisting you on this flight. Would you care for something to drink before we depart, Miss Jones?"

Sadie was slow to respond, but before the woman asked again, she mustered a raspy "No."

The attendant walked back up the aisle of the jet, where she tended to the lone man sitting in one of four, creamy-white leather seats surrounding a table made of burled walnut. Across the aisle was a sofa made of the same sumptuous leather; rich accents highlighted the opulence which was unabashedly on display throughout the jet's cabin.

Sadie studied the man's gestures. He seemed unsettled; repeatedly rattling the ice against his empty glass before lifting it to his ready lips. Over and over again, he tried to drain another drop of liquor from the stubborn cubes.

Finally, the flight attendant filled the crystal tumbler with another pour of whiskey. She then softly announced to him, "Wheels up in 10, sir."

Sadie rubbed her eyes and pulled back on her wild tresses to study her surroundings. While the extravagance of the luxury jet did not escape her, she was much more curious about the passenger up front.

She tried to get a better look at him each time he anxiously pivoted his chair toward the aisle then back toward the window; never quite turning enough for her to get a meaningful glimpse. All the while his sight was locked onto whatever was happening outside his jet window. If only he would turn that damn seat around enough for Sadie to make out his face. He stopped swiveling and leaned closer into the window, then impatiently asked, "Any word from the others?"

In an instant, Sadie was served an emotional cocktail of shock and relief as she recognized the voice. She called out, "Ali?! Ali, is that *you*?" The revelation sobered her up quickly. She unfastened the seatbelt and pushed herself off the cushion, but before Sadie could straighten up, she was approached from behind by two very attentive men. They were the same two thugs from the car ride—the ones assigned "to protect" her.

The mystery man up front, Ali, immediately turned to the men, signaling them to stand down. "No, no, it's fine. Let her come up front with me," he said as he grabbed the starched, white, collar of his shirt and gave it a couple of good, hard, tugs to release the choke. He took one last swig of his whiskey then stood up to receive Sadie.

Ali was a power house of brains and brawn. His 6'2" stature was cool and capable; U.S. military training—Delta Force—made sure of that.

Sadie broke herself free from the men and ran to Ali. She threw herself into his protective embrace, as he hugged her, like a once lost child. Then, her questions fired from her lips in a peppered barrage, "Where's my dad? Have you been by the house, Ali? Where is he? Is he alright!? Oh god, our house! It's engulfed with fire and smoke and the police are there…and then these men came and they hauled me away, and they drugged me with something. What is going on? Christ, Ali. Why are we here?!!" Sadie was grabbing and shaking Ali's arm before she broke down into sobbing tears; concerned for her father's safety, confused about her own, yet thankful to see a familiar face.

Ali wrapped his arm around Sadie and guided her to the seat across the table from his own. His eyes shifted away from hers in hopes of evading Sadie's questions. It did not work. Relentlessly, she turned up the heat. "Ali, we have to find Dad. Let's go. Let's go, now!"

Ali cringed with each call for her father, then in a heated burst he slammed his hand on the table and shouted, "Sadie, Sadie! Cassandra!!" Ali had never been abrupt with her before; his training, had always been a shield for his true emotions, in the past. He fell back in line, then evenly stated, "Calm down, everything is under control," as he turned his attention back to the jet window; seeking confirmation for his own words. "Trust me," he said, unconvincingly, placing his hand atop Sadie's and giving it a tight squeeze; realizing he was far too invested in this mission.

Sadie retreated, back into the seat without breaking the line of sight between herself and Ali. She had always trusted him—like her own father. She let her mind drift backwards, over the ocean of time, with the two men who had guarded her life as though theirs depended on it.

Ali and her father had met early on, in the military--75th Ranger Regiment. They moved up the ranks together, through JSOC (Joint Special Operations Command). Until one day, Ali was recruited by "The Unit" -- Delta Force. Rumor had it that her father took it hard at first; he wanted it more than Ali. But throughout their military careers they had remained tight. They seemed inseparable, even when Ali would disappear on top secret missions for weeks at a time, he managed to find some way to check in with us.

Sadie's father, Jack "Cannibal" Jones, was more of a lone wolf. He was very low-keyed, kept mostly to himself except for his frequent meetups with Ali.

Jack was tagged with the nickname "Cannibal" by a young soldier in his unit and it stuck with him for the rest of his military career. It referred to Jack's skillful ability to take workable parts from a fallen helicopter and use them to make another bird fly. He honed this skill, during his many stints in the Persian Gulf, a couple decades back.

He flew clandestine missions over the desert, repeatedly, up until the time he got shot down. After that, his missions stopped suddenly, and he played the role of a retiree; he wasn't very good at it. He continued with "special assignments" every few weeks, where he would lock himself behind the doors of secrecy for many hours before emerging, exhausted and hungry.

Sadie never knew much about what exactly happened with her father while he was in the Persian desert or behind the closed doors of secrecy at home. All she knew for sure, was that his last mission was classified "Top Secret." The redacted file was now a sanitized version, stating only that he "was missing in action" for some time, then "extricated from the scene" once located. Her father never spoke about it either, no matter how much Sadie pressed him for details.

The flight attendant barged into Sadie's trip down memory lane with another update. This time her tone was much more urgent as she let Ali know, "Wheels up in less than 5, sir. Is there a message you would like me to pass to the captain?" As she reminded Ali of the diminishing time before take-off; the whine of the engines whirling up increased the tension in the cabin.

Ali's usual unflinching calm was again irritated by the delayed arrival, as he spoke, more so to reassure himself, "Tell...uh, the captain, we must wait. I know he'll be here."

Sadie picked up what Ali just dropped, "Who'll be here? My dad? Did he escape the fire? Is he coming? Here?" She leaned into the window, searching for any sign of her father. When he didn't appear, she badgered Ali once again, "Why are we on this plane anyway? Whose plane is this? Where are we all going?" Sadie had regained most of the bravery and grit Ali had come to admire in her over the years. Just as she began pushing harder for answers; Ali suddenly shot up from his seat.

"He's here!" Ali informed the flight attendant as he jumped to his feet, watching the black sedan pull around the left side of the plane. He ran out of sight, through the jet door and down the stairs to the approaching car.

Sadie attempted to follow him but the guards immediately let her know to stay put. She turned and twisted toward the entrance of the jet to get a glimpse of her father, but she could not see anything from her seat. She turned again, this time toward the window in another attempt to gain view, but to no avail. Frustrated, she once again, jumped up from her seat and turned toward the jet door in one swift move, when she was met with the cold, black-eyed stare of a man standing almost seven feet tall. Her dainty nose was so close to him that she could feel her own breath repel off his chest.

Sadie gasped in horror at the initial sight, but quickly began questioning the man with contempt, "You again?! Where's my father?" She tried to shove him aside to get around him but he was strong and threatening as he blocked her passage. She screamed out, "Ali! Ali, do you have

Dad!?" She attempted to squirm around the brute one more time before he single-handedly rooted her deep into the seat.

He walked around to the opposite side of the table and made himself comfortable in the seat Ali had occupied just a moment ago. "Buckle up," he said, with little emotion, as the jet door was being secured. With a loud snap of his fingers, he motioned to the flight attendant to remove Ali's whiskey glass. His nostrils flared with judgement; the smell of alcohol insulted his senses.

She obeyed.

Sadie's mind fell into a tailspin of questions: *What just happened? Where is Ali? Someone wake me up from this nightmare!* She opened her mouth to demand answers once again, only to be met with a brusque motion for silence from the vile one's hand.

Wrought by his presence, Sadie cowered into the background. She quietly moved closer to the jet window for one last desperate search for her father and Ali to come to her rescue. No one came.

The G7 began its slow roll; pulling away from the private hangar. The jet made a tight turn onto the runway.

Then, through each of the windows along the body of the jet, Sadie caught momentary glimpses of the black sedan pulling away. She bobbed her head from window to window in order to keep the car in sight. Its red taillights disappeared as it made a turn onto the access road and picked up speed; leaving Sadie in its dust.

She wanted to close her eyes and faint away but her mind was vigilant; refusing to accept what her vision was receiving. *How could Ali abandon me here? Did he leave to get help? Why would he allow the vile one onboard?* Her questions failed to shed any light.

Sadie was now a prisoner; terror and betrayal were her cellmates. It felt like the walls were closing in on her. *I can't breathe, I can't breathe* she repeated to herself as her fate was sealed with the disappearance of the sedan. Ali had driven off with her freedom in tow.

The distorted voice of the captain announced, "Ready for take-off." His words were garbled and full of static; muffled by the engine noise as the jet gained speed upon the runway. Sadie tightened her seatbelt; it was the only semblance of security she had left. These men were taking her away from everything she had known for the past eighteen years. Her life, as she had known it, had been hijacked.

Ta-ting-ting. Ta-ting-ting. The incessant clatter of the crystal tumblers, nervously riding out the long runway prompted Sadie to look back into the galley. The noise began to taper once the jet lifted off the ground. The steep climb seemed to last forever before the aircraft leveled off and headed out, over the Atlantic.

Sadie continued to look back into the galley; turning further till she saw Faith buckled into the jump seat closest to the exit. Faith was overtly nervous, biting her once perfectly

manicured nails, as she stared out at the fleeting clouds
through her tiny window.

Sadie tried to capture Faith's attention by sheer will.
Finally, Faith turned her view inward, toward the aisle of the
jet, before they locked eyes. Sadie then initiated a silent yet
expressive appeal for help. Her plea did not go unnoticed.

Powerless, Faith gave one negating side-to-side motion
with her head, then she quickly looked away; eager to
preserve her own delicate neck.

With his thick foreign accent, the vile one spoke again,
"You should sit back, relax. This is going to be a long night
for you." He gestured for Sadie to turn around and lean back
into the seat as he once again indulged himself in her,
visually. After a lengthy viewing, the voyeur's gaze turned
to the satchel he had carried onto the jet with him. He
reached into the bag and pulled out a long black silk scarf.
He threw it across the table towards Sadie as he barked out,

"Cover your hair!" He demanded it; acting offended by her unabashed display of beauty.

Rattled, she submitted to his command. Sadie took the scarf with one hand as she tamed her long curls with the other.

Before she had a chance to wrap the silk around her head he spewed at her once more. "Turn away when you do this. Have you no shame?" The vile one stood in disgust, grabbed his satchel, and headed to the back of the jet. He ducked his towering stature through a doorway that had gone unnoticed by Sadie up until that moment.

She leaned slightly into the aisle as her sight followed him back into the private room. Before she could see inside, the door slammed shut; deflecting her focus toward the two clocks hanging directly above the doorway. Written beneath each clock was the designated location for its respective time. The first label read, "Washington, DC," the second, "Tehran, Iran!"

## Chapter Four

Crash! The sudden noise awakened Sadie to a new destination. A lone crystal tumbler had escaped its leather restraint and fallen to the floorboard of the jet upon landing. The delicate vessel shattered; the shards of glass scattered and hid as the jet bumped along the concrete runway. It took a long time before the jet pulled up and stopped on the sticky tarmac.

The moment the engines were silenced the heat from the midday sun began to penetrate the thin metal shell of the luxury jet. Sadie peered out of the window at the foreign land. A dark blanket of city soot concealed the Persian blue sky, morphing the city into a darkened state. In the distance, heat waves persisted in their sultry dance above the blacktop.

They were mesmerizing Sadie, as if a mystic veil was being pulled over her eyes.

She sat in unwelcomed surrender, staring out of the jet window. A solitary tear burst through the feigned wall of strength she had managed to build along her outer edge. The drop rolled down her face and into her lap. Unclasping her hands from their tight prayerful grip; she quickly wiped her cheek of any remains of the salty traitor.

"Excuse me, Miss Jones, I'm sorry but we must hurry," Reza, one of the guards who had been watching over her throughout the night, required Sadie's attention, "You will have to secure the head scarf tighter than that Miss." He tried to show her without laying his hands upon her tresses. "Your hair, Miss Jones, will have to be completely covered now that we've arrived." He pointed out of the jet window to a sign that read, IMAM KHOMEINI INTERNATIONAL AIRPORT – TEHRAN. He reinforced his request, "It's the law of the land."

Upon reading the sign, Sadie confirmed her fears—she had been abducted to Iran—*but why her? Why here?* Her thoughts plunged into the darkness of the past twenty-four hours once again.

As she looked out onto the foreign land, she viewed the fence line surrounding the airport where she saw a restrained but growing crowd of protestors. The mass was focused on the luxury jet. They swarmed in like moths attracted to light. Their loud chanting reverberated through the hull of the plane. Sadie couldn't understand the words but she could feel their intensity. The people were waving signs and banners in erratic and lunging movements as they roared their beliefs through the barrier.

Private security guards, a dozen or more, were on the ground ready to protect the jet and its contents. Each guard was heavily armed with a Russian-made AK-47. The threat of being bashed in the head with the butt-end of a Kalashnikov seemed to be enough to keep the crowd from climbing over the fence; yet their persistent chanting continued in waves as they pushed and pulled upon the metal mesh.

Reza tugged at the tip of Sadie's scarf once again, asking for compliance with his request. She obediently tucked away every wild curl and tied the scarf into a tight knot under her chin. She snuck another look at the growing mob then pulled the scarf down to her eyebrows and secured it tightly against her forehead. She looked up to the guards for approval. Reza smiled with an affirming nod that comforted Sadie for a flickering moment. These men, whom she had vehemently fought against hours before, were now the very ones she turned to for protection.

Turning her troubled gaze back to the chanting crowd, she asked, "What are they shouting? Why are they so angry?"

Reza looked at the mob. With a silent vow of support, he calmly stated, "The path to freedom is forged by fire," as he pointed to a hand painted sign, scribbled in English, that was barely noticeable from between the Perso-Arabic script written upon the sea of hand-made signs.

"Fire? Do they want to torch the plane?" Sadie asked with sarcasm fueled by stress. She reached for Reza's arm and pulled herself up to him in hopes of getting an encouraging response to her question.

Before he could answer, the vile one emerged from his private quarters. Upon seeing the interaction between Reza and Sadie he immediately rushed toward them. Inches away from Reza's face he cautioned, "Do not cross the boundaries of your job!" He pushed the guard away from Sadie, demanding distance from her. Sauntering down the aisle toward the cockpit he turned to fire commands back at Reza, "I've been informed that the captain will have to come with us. Do you understand?" He glared at Reza to make sure he understood the change in plans around the captain's movement. "You have your orders."

Reza nodded.

Once again, the vile one barked, "Do we have clearance, yet? What are we waiting for? We need to move, now!" His voice boomed throughout the cabin as he impatiently slammed his fist against the exit door of the jet.

As if by his command the jet door was finally permitted to be unlatched and opened by the guards on the ground. A blast of fiery-hot air rushed into the cabin. The gust was dusty and dry; it dispensed sand and debris into the pristine crevices of the luxury jet.

Sadie instantly gagged on the smell of raw garbage and body odor that had infiltrated the plane. "Holy cow what is that?" she asked between dry heaves. The query was left wafting beneath the blanket of stench as the security detail swiftly took control of the exposed cabin. Their motions were fast and skilled. They signaled to each other before deploying the assets into place; providing the highest level of protection around Sadie. It was clear Reza was now in charge as he maneuvered Sadie to the jet door; shielding her from the exposed exit with his own body. Quickly, everyone received final instructions. Reza showed Sadie where to position herself, behind and to the right of him at all times.

He called out, "Don't move ahead or to the left. No matter what, do not stop. Keep walking, head down, out of the jet, across the tarmac, past the guard gate then through the glass doors." He pointed directly to a set of electronic doors with Arabic script written above the entrance. Beneath the writing were two arrows--one directing 'Iranians' the other 'Foreigners.'

Reza looked at Sadie, right into her wide-eyed stare and clarified once more, "Just stay in position, look down and walk! Do not say a word. Do you understand?"

Sadie nodded her head nervously agreeing to obey every word of his explicit orders.

"Let's move!" Reza led the group, single file and single-minded on delivering the treasure, unharmed, as ordered.

They proceeded through the jet door and down the stairs. First in the line of fire was Reza, pointing his weapon from left to right and back again. Sadie was fast on his heels, with the vile one and the flight crew following close behind, but out of her periphery. The second guard was tightly watching all their backs; as was the security detail on the ground.

The moment Sadie's foot touched the tarmac the crowd began shouting out, "Attisheh ma! Attisheh ma!"

Distracted, Sadie stopped and looked up in response to the outcry. The vile one's proximity propelled her forward as the rear guard began yelling to Sadie, "Move it, move it, move it!" He was angered yet ever protective of her as the anxious crowd wanted more than Sadie's attention.

They ran to the gate where Reza surreptitiously handed a rolled wad of 'Benjamins' to a uniformed Iranian military guard. Cash was still king in these parts, and it opened this door without any trouble. The officer lifted the barricade with a quick nod to Reza; allowing each of them passage, without a spoken word.

As the electronic doors swished open, Sadie was aghast by the multitude. The crowd was forceful; undulating as one massive body. Chained links and armed guards were intermittently providing a narrow path through which Reza maneuvered the group. With each step, the crowd swarmed forward; refusing to give up their newly captured ground as they pushed in closer for their fierce welcome.

Sadie gripped Reza's belt tighter with both hands as she was being jerked through the masses. Beads of sweat entered and burned her eyes. She was determined to stay with her bodyguard as they cut through the mayhem to the street side of the airport building. Once outside, the dry desert wind was now a sign of freedom from the crowd.

Reza rushed Sadie to the curb, where five black, Range Rovers were staggered; restraining incoming traffic to the airport. Horns were frantically sounding from the line of cars, buses and taxis that were quickly building up behind the blockade. In front of the row of SUVs, was a black Mercedes-Benz S600 limo—fully armored.

Reza moved Sadie toward the Benz. He signaled the door to be opened then buckled her into the right rear seat. He flashed hand signals to the driver then, everything seemed to happen all at once. Reza began securing the others into their SUVs. Faith was escorted to the first taxi in line and allowed to leave down the service road. Sadie turned back, and watched the vile one enter the last vehicle on his own accord. The guards split up and entered the vehicles which moved into position, flanking the Benz.

As Reza rushed the captain into the last vehicle, a sudden gust of hot desert wind blasted through; blowing the captain's hat clear off. It was a reflex that made the captain juggle to catch the tumbling hat before he hurriedly climbed in beside the vile one. The last thing Sadie witnessed was the flash of the captain's face before the door slammed shut. She cried out in disbelief, "Dad!!?"

Chapter Five


The Benz effortlessly reached high speeds. The crimson and gold insignia flags atop the front fenders allowed the black caravan to pass unhindered as they quickly cleared Tehran's city limits. The changing power had already influenced control over the city, but they had learned from history that one must also win the hearts of the peasants of the land in order to stake claim over the treasures of the entire kingdom. So off they sped, to the heart of the old country.

All the while, Sadie had been beating her fists against the privacy panel of the limo, attempting to get Reza's attention; she wanted out. She then screamed at the driver; her 'request' was not heeded. She desperately wanted to talk to her father to find out what the hell was going on, but she was sealed inside the armored car with no way of reaching him, even as his SUV followed close behind the Benz.

Ahead lay at least six hours of driving along the desolate highway. Sadie repeatedly looked back to see if her father's vehicle was still in sight. She was exhausted. Yet, through blood-shot eyes she continued to survey the barren land through which the caravan passed. For miles and miles all she could see were red clay hills with modest villages tucked between them. The old Persian valley was long and sparsely dotted with shrubs and trees. The only sign of life, between the distant villages, was the periodic spiral of sand whirling in mystic circles upon the desert. Sadie witnessed the helpless grains being picked up at whim by the far-reaching wind before being coerced to dance. Their movement became hypnotic as Sadie brooded over her fate.

## Chapter Six

Jack threw the pilot's cap onto the seat next to him as he undid the buttons of his collar. Frustrated, he bellowed at the vile one, "What the hell happened to the plan, Akbar? Where is Ali?" He leaned forward to yell at the driver, "Turn up the damn A.C.!" The vein at his jugular bulged as he turned his attention back to Akbar. "Well?!"

Akbar was stern yet calm in his response, "We had a flare up at the fire scene. Ali had to circle back and make sure it was, uh, shall we say, 'contained'."

The ridges in Jack's brow line furled, he became more annoyed. "What do mean a flare up? That house burned clean—it will be reported as 'faulty wiring;' no trace left behind. *Our* guys don't leave loose ends." He leaned toward the center console to keep an eye on his prized possession in the car ahead.

"It's not the house fire, Jack. Apparently, she has a suitor, a persistent young bastard who saw us pick her up. He was asking questions and drawing the attention of the police working crowd control around the fire." Akbar then extended his left pinky which had a long, yellow, finger nail protruding, almost an inch, from its end. He used it to pick at his earwax before flicking away the meager findings. "Don't worry yourself. We have had our plans in place for almost twenty years now, Jack. You don't think this gnat is going to derail us, do you? The boy is a nuisance; he hasn't even come up on surveillance, he is nothing, a nobody; Ali will put an end to it."

Jack's eyes began darting left and right, you could almost see the inner workings of his mind; he hated changes to a plan in motion. "You goddam well better be right. I've been babysitting this golden egg for far too long; given up most of my freakin' life for her. I'm not about to let--"

"I said, it will be contained!" Akbar forced the end to this discussion. He still held the upper hand.

Chapter Seven

Dusk led the way into the village; painting the streets in vibrant orange and purple hues reflected by the setting sun. The caravan crested the road leading into the sprawling town. The once distant, Tower of Silence, now stood obscured by the structures that had steadily advanced across the land, over the past eighteen years of growth.

Jack silently peered out of the car window. He nervously cracked the joints of his neck as his mind reeled back in time to the images of the violent mission he led here. He closed his eyes and shook his head as if to shake off the memories.

As they entered the city limits, Jack felt a cold chill penetrate his spine; he shuddered when the vehicle passed through the shadow of the Tower of Silence. He once again sensed the surge of a mystic presence surround him. He had never quite managed to escape it, not completely. He sunk deeper, into the seat, attempting to hide from the intruding energy.

Akbar amused himself with Jack's unease. He thought this tension could use a little provocation, so he pointed his crooked, hairy finger at the dark, stone structure and began baiting, "Do you know what that is, the old tower? This one, right here." He did not wait for Jack to respond. "There was a time when this land was ruled by Magi, so-called 'sages of ancient wisdom' who thought themselves to be wiser than you and I, Jack."

Jack wiped the sweat from his brow as he turned to look back at the looming structure.

"These men, the sages, they used to climb the steepest mountains, hold secret meetings in caves and they worshipped fire!" Akbar said with an over-acted tone of incredulity as he continued, "So much so that they would never consider cremation of their departed loved ones. No, no, *their* dead were placed atop that tower. The dead spent many days exposed to the sun and to scavenging birds that picked incessantly at those rotting bodies." He paused, to relish in the sickened expression on Jack's face.

Jack moved to change the subject away from his one vulnerability--anything that had to do with this mystic, magic, voodoo mumbo jumbo--even a highly-trained, ex-military man, had difficulty controlling what he refused to understand. Jack snapped his fingers and pointed down the road a ways, turning the conversation in a new direction, "There, there it is! Finally, we are here." He could make out the darkness of the iron gates between the light stones of the protective walls. The entrance led to a massive network of underground tunnels beneath the once-holy grounds. He fell back in time again recalling to himself, *All those Army boys swearing the whole time they were digging this place. We couldn't wait until all the tunnels were finished so we could work underground, away from the penetrating rays of sunlight. They couldn't wait to finish the job and get the hell out of this shit hole.*

The caravan stopped in front of the enormous gates as they slowly creaked open, one at a time. Jack could almost feel their weight on his chest. He peered up at them as the caravan passed through, one by one. The gates shut, tight behind them. The quietness was deafening as the vehicles entered the first of many tunnels that led deep underground.

The complex was intertwined into the very land where the Magi once stood and shared their wisdom. One part of their old home remained to this day as a cornerstone for the palace where Sadie was to be delivered.

From the outside, the newly constructed buildings kept a very modest appearance in order to appeal to the sensibilities of the current leaders attending mosque nearby. But make no mistake, once inside the walled compound, and deep beneath the tunneled interiors, this palace was built for a king.

A monarch was about to be placed upon a throne of gold. The deed was being handled by the world's most calculating powers. They had hand-chosen their young and very eager puppet decades ago and groomed him into the role.

The future king had spent the last several years understanding everything that is expected of him--which was not much. In his spare time, he spent days calculating his future compensation for following orders. He impatiently waited to take his seat as the ruler of the land, alongside his soon-to-be bride, of whose beauty he had heard mere rumors, but was given a small picture taken of her a few years ago, at the age of 14. He thought her to be quite the perfect trophy; one befitting his kinghood.

It had been Jack's job to make sure nothing got in the way of this plan; but now, with Jack being exposed to Sadie at the airport, he feverishly entered damage-control mode. He held back his anger as he began reasoning with Akbar, "I need to see her; she's too smart to let this slide for too long.

She will be demanding some explanations and soon! It must be me; she will not trust any one of you, since you let Ali stay back. No way will she give in to anyone else; not until she finds out that I'm OK and that she's OK, and she actually speaks with me. I witnessed it, in her expression, as the blanket of trust, I had worked so hard to weave over the past 18 years, unraveled in that moment, that her eyes told her that her own father had flown her into this shithole. She will demand answers."

Akbar is bewildered at how a woman, let alone this dainty, young Sadie, could affect such a reaction in this 'big, strong, man'. He looked away in disgust.

Jack's eyes darted back and forth quickly, searching for the right actions. He always hated changes during a mission. He pressed on, "She will only accept her role in this if it comes from me; even then, it will be a battle of wills. I'm the one she's trusted for the past eighteen years; I know her character. I'm telling you, no one in this country can get through to her, not now, not after what we've just put her through. I must be the one to give her the news, and it has to be soon!"

"In time Jack, in time. Be a little patient, you have waited this long," Akbar was calm yet deliberate in his delivery. "Besides, she must be cleansed before she can enter 'His Excellency's' presence," he said with a snide grin, at the insincere distinction he bestowed upon the puppet king. With a deep sigh, he stated, "We have time yet;" fondling his beard while secretly visiting Sadie's beauty in his own mind, yet again.

# Chapter Eight

Sadie had been escorted from the limo through dimly light corridors before entering an expansive bedroom suite. She was guided to a set of chairs and a small table in the center of the voluminous room which had the biggest bed Sadie had even seen, perched upon a raised floor, with three granite steps leading up to it. The suite was richly adorned with lavish silk rugs, satin beddings, velvet drapes and giant stone columns. It looked medieval in design yet fresh and new in construction. Sadie took in every detail.

She walked around the entire suite; half in awe, half looking for a way out.

The walls of the main room were cut from large stones and built into a circular tower with small rectangular windows around the entire upper circumference. The windows seemed useless as they were placed over thirty feet above the floor; too high to get a view of the outside, yet they allowed the most beautiful rays of light to converge into the center of the room.

Sadie was drawn to the light.

She stood on a crimson and gold hand-woven rug, in the middle of the grand room. Looking up, she noticed the round window at the apex of the tower's dome, where the light poured in from the rising full moon. The moon beams showered upon her entire being and gently kissed her face, as dust particles danced and swirled within the light. A sense of serenity encircled Sadie; she welcomed it. Then Sadie took in one, long, deep, breath and slowly let it escape.

"I feel like a bird..." she whispered, then looked around at the magnificence of her surroundings, "...in a gilded cage."

Her focus returned to finding a way out. Sadie knew her father was close; she watched the motorcade of Range Rovers that followed her all the way here. She proceeded to nose around; planning to open doors to see where they might lead.

When starting with the one she entered through, she was disappointed upon being addressed by two armed and foreboding guards, posted right outside. She excused herself and quickly shut the door, backing away and moving across the room to another door that looked like it might be promising. She put her ear against the door to see if she could hear anyone out there. Then ever so gently she wrapped her fingers around the door handle, just as she was about to engage it, the door flung open and a woman carrying a huge tray of fresh fruit, dates, figs, nuts, and cucumbers came rushing in, like a whirlwind.

"Oh! Excuse me!" Sadie said as a reflex, while being hurled back against the wall by the momentum of the opening door.

The woman was covered, from head to toe with a long, black cloth, a veil--hijab, that she managed to keep closely wrapped around her ample figure as she quickly waddled across the room. By securing the fabric tightly between her teeth, framing her almond eyes and ruddy cheeks, she was able to keep her hands free, as she placed the silver tray on the round table near the center of the room. She bowed repeatedly towards Sadie while waddling backwards through the doorway from which she had entered, smiling with her eyes the whole way.

Sadie was about to peer into the doorway when the woman came rushing back, pleasantly nodding her head repeatedly towards Sadie, then placing small plates and a paring knife by the fruit. She knelt, on the floor close to the tray and began peeling one of the tiny Persian cucumbers.

The cool fresh scent aroused Sadie's hunger. Next, the woman sliced into the deep, purple, flesh of a plump, ripe plum as Sadie watched the pink nectar spill away.

Sadie's mouth watered at the sight, "Oh man, that smells so good!" The sweetness of the fruit perfumed the entire room. "Would you mind if I grabbed a couple?" Sadie reached over and grabbed two plums and a fig, and took a few steps back to devour the fruit. The juices dripped from her lips and onto the silk rug she had been sharing with the moonlight just a few moments ago. "Jeez, I'm such a slob; sorry. You brought in plates for us to use and I'm over here squirting juice all over the place! What a mess!" Sadie bent down to clean up the plum juices when, all of a sudden...

"Nah, nah, nah!" The woman squealed, mortified that Sadie would stoop in her presence. Her hijab dropped to the floor when she opened her mouth for the loud yelp. She grabbed a linen napkin from the tray and fervently dabbed at the sticky drops. As she wiped the rug with one hand, she gestured to her own chest with the other; attempting to inform Sadie that it is her pleasure to take care of this. "I do, I do!" She looked up at Sadie with her now very visible smile; tickled to have released the tight hold her teeth had on the veil covering her body.

Sadie was surprised to hear a word she understood in this foreign place. She wiped her hands on her dress and helped the woman up by the arm, leading her to a seat close to the fruit. "Come. Sit. Please," she stated while pointing at the chair repeatedly.

The woman brushed herself off, straightened her skirt and stood with clasped hands, continually nodding her head with obeisance to whatever Sadie asked, while anxiously looking around to see if anyone was watching.

"Sit, please, enjoy some fruit with me." Sadie laughed under her breath, wondering why her own speech had become stilted and broken as if English was *her* second language. Then she gently gestured, once again, in the direction of the chair.

The woman nervously took a seat, as directed. She was unsure of herself but delighted by the invitation at the same time. She looked at Sadie with the excitement of a child who was about to enter a candy store for the very first time.

Sadie did not know if the woman understood a word she was saying. "So...do-you-speak-English?" she asked in a hopeful tone.

"A little; I study with my...eh, um...uncle. When I help him at the....eh, eh...bazaar." She shakes off the word, as she knows she can do better. "The shop, the shop...I go when he need me for help him." She giggled at her own accomplishment of carrying a real-life conversation in English.

"Wonderful! What is your name?" Sadie encouraged, hoping to get some information from this woman.

"My name is Mahtab. It means, Moonlight," she said, again filled with joy.

"Mahtab, what a lovely name. It is a pleasure to meet you. I am Cassandra or Sadie if that is easier."

As soon as Sadie introduced herself, Mahtab's brow furled, then her eyes widened and she jumped to her feet as if a fire had been lit beneath her seat. Mahtab walked away backwards, again, as she bowed repeatedly hastening her exit from the room.

"Wait! Can you stay a while and chat? I want to know where I am. Mahtab, come back!" Sadie was frustrated and confused but too exhausted to do anything about it. She ate more fruit and nuts while continuing to investigate the suite and its contents, as she wondered to herself, *what next?*

With her hunger satisfied she found herself desperate to close her eyes, if only for a few minutes. She walked over to the sumptuous bed; it held the promise of sleep between its layers of satin, silk, and feathers. Sadie sat upon the bed;

sinking into its soft, billowy comfort. It did not take long before she fell out of her nightmare and into a deep sleep.

Chapter Nine

Whispers and chattering were trespassing into Sadie's dreams before she was forced to open her eyes. The dry desert air had crusted them shut while she had slept through the entire night, under the blanket of pure exhaustion. She lifted her head and reluctantly pried one eyelid open, then the next. As she looked down the length of her body, splayed out on the bed, she laughed at her shoes, half dangling from her feet. She then looked beyond, to the blurry figures behind the chattering. The women slowly came into focus; Mahtab had returned, and brought along a few friends.

The four women were standing against the far wall of the bedroom suite, talking amongst themselves as they watched Sadie sleep. They had wheeled in a golden cart, with lush, white towels, perfumes, bath oils and jugs and jugs of milk, upon it.

Sadie twisted and stretched herself upright as she rubbed the last of the sleep from her eyes. As if on que, the women rushed to Sadie and surrounded her as they proceeded to remove her shoes and unzip her dress, while rhythmically whispering "Attisheh ma" as if chanting a prayer.

When they attempted to remove her dress, Sadie objected, "Hey, hey wait a minute, what are you doing?" She was flustered and embarrassed but naked soon enough, except for the long white silk sheet that Mahtab managed to modestly wrap around Sadie's now curled up body. She sat, balled up in silk, pushing herself back to the very top of the bed...there was nowhere else to go.

Two of the women scurried into the enormous bathroom where they proceeded to fill a huge, step-down tub, hewn from a solid piece of granite.

With a little gentle coaxing, Sadie was led into the bathroom.

"This isn't a bathroom, it's a *spa*! Look at that tub…it's the size of a swimming pool!" Sadie exclaimed as she backed against the wall to watch the women work. One would drop scented oil into the pool of water while another emptied the many jugs of milk into the tub and then dripped ribbons of honey atop the water. As a final touch, they sprinkled pink and white rose petals into the bath before motioning Sadie to come over to them.

"Come. We wash." Mahtab beckoned.

Sadie is looking around, wondering how much longer they are all going to hang out together; while, all she wanted to do was to get out, find her dad, and a way back home.

Once again, Mahtab gently insisted, "You come. We wash. Now."

Sadie held the silk wrap tightly in place with one hand, while lifting the other hand in protest, "Look, I love the spa treatment, but what I really need right now are some answers. I've been pushed and pulled around for the past day and night, ripped from my life as I knew it; is anyone going to tell me what is going on?"

Sadie's question was responded by Mahtab pointing to the bath water. "Please. Come in, eh…go in. Please, get in water!"

Sadie rolled her eyes and moved toward the bath. With each step down into the warm embrace of milk and honey, Mahtab would discreetly lift the draped silk away from Sadie's bare body; never allowing her nakedness to be revealed. Once submerged, the women went to work. All hands were on Sadie; scrubbing, rubbing, oiling, shampooing, clipping, and sloughing every inch of her body.

"Assault with a soapy sponge!" Sadie nervously joked out loud before finally resigning herself to the pampering.

The warm water felt wonderful against her skin. Sadie could not see her body amidst the milk and honey concoction, but she could feel its magic working on her tense muscles. After the women were done, Sadie stayed in the soothing bath until the waters cooled. She was then rinsed with golden bowls, filled with tepid water infused with rose oil, before being led up the steps of the deep bath to be dried.

As the ladies passed towels to Mahtab, Sadie asked about their chanting, "Mahtab, I've heard this call at the airport, and now you all are saying it, over and over. What does it mean, and why is everyone saying it at the same time, across the airport and now here? This, 'A-tishay-mow'?"

"Attisheh ma." Mahtab gently corrected Sadie.

"Yes, that's it...attisheh ma."

"You are our Light." Mahtab said, as her eyes welled up with tears. "You are the Light of our light my princess!" Mahtab expressed, once again, bowing her head to Sadie.

"Phhft...that's a beautiful saying, but, uh...I'm no princess; ask anyone, let's start with my Dad! Where is he? He's tall, thin, reddish-brown hair..." Sadie prodded, still unsure of everything that is happening, yet she welcomed the kindness and warmth of these women.

Mahtab looked up at Sadie as she knelt at her feet with one of the plush, drying towels. "Oh! But you are our princess, our princess of Light; you no can hide this truth. I now see with my own eyes, and I have three peoples. They see too." She dries Sadie's upper thigh with the thirsty towel as she stops to look into Sadie's eyes, knowingly. "You, see? Here?" she said pointing to Sadie's birthmark. The same one that Sadie had spent years trying to cover up in her youth.

Sadie laughed, out loud this time. "Are you talking about *this*? My birthmark? The ol' goblet-of-fire?" Which was how she referred to the mark that was shaped like an ancient vessel with a constant breath of fire escaping its spout. Embarrassed she covered the mark with her hand. "What does my ugly birthmark have to do with anything?" She lifted one side of her hand from her thigh to examine the mark again. "It's been here since I was born. There's nothing I can do about it."

Mahtab shook her head and stood up. She slipped a smooth, silk robe around Sadie and mysteriously stated, "The Light of this lamp will show you the way, when the time is right."

Just then, a loud and persistent knocking at the door interrupted their conversation. Mahtab quickly gathered all that they had brought with them, and rushed out of the room. Leaving Sadie, alone, to answer the call.

## Chapter Ten

RAP, RAP, RAP…*RAP, RAP, RAP*…The intruder was incessant. The knocks on the door got louder and faster as if the morning-caller was angered at having to wait for Sadie.

She hesitated, then headed toward the door. Before she could reach it, the door opened part way as the voice snapped out sharply, "It's alright, it's alright, she is expecting me!" he lied to the men standing at guard, as he pushed himself into the room, slamming the door shut behind himself.

Akbar walked into the palatial suite, commanding authority, while watching Sadie adjust the silk robe around her body, tightly. It was her only protection between the vile one and herself.

"You don't quite understand the point of the knock, do you?!" Sadie was not surprised, but she was angered, by the sight of him. The fearless Sadie, that Ali always had encouraged, was present at this moment as she fired away, "I had hoped you would have crawled back to the rock under which you slithered out!"

She backed away from him, but continued her attack, "I saw you with my father. You know where he is! Take me to him!"

He walked over to the round table, picked up the paring knife and a bright, orange peach and slowly sliced into its delicate flesh without watching what he was doing. His stare did not waver from Sadie as he matter-of-factly stated, "You need to learn some manners. You are not in America... 'you are not in Kansas anymore'."

He threw the peach segments onto the tray and began using the knife to pick beneath his finger nails. "Sit down," he said, using the knife to point to the chair. When Sadie did not follow his instruction he demanded, "Sit. Down!"

Sadie once again let fear control the moment. She did as she was told.

Akbar walked behind her chair and stood close enough that she could smell his disgusting breath. He gave her a little sugar, the words she desperately wanted to hear, "Yes, I know where your father is. You will hear from him soon enough." Then, he delivered the whip of words she loathed, "But first, you and I need to come to an understanding."

All Sadie could do was shake her head 'no.' She was so repulsed by every aspect of this man, except one…he knew where her father was being held. Grudgingly she asked, "What? What is it you want? What could you and I possibly come together to understand?" She twisted around to stare *him* down. Then boldly mocking him, she stated, "Sit down. Explain yourself."

Akbar let her slide on that one; he knew what he was about to say would be enough to put her back in her place. Gesturing in a wide sweeping motion to the lavish suite he asked, "Did you think all this is for you?" He grinned, without waiting for a response as he continued, "You will be required to make some effort in exchange for what we are doing for you."

"*For* me? How about, what you are doing *to* me?"

He kept on without giving her a response, "We will provide this beautiful palace, and you will do as you are instructed, for as long as we require, in order to complete your duty--'for the good of the people'."

Sadie heard the smugness in his voice. She was in a state of heightened awareness, her eyes shifted back and forth, searching for help, but finding none. "I'm not interested in helping the likes of *you*, or your people!"

There was an *almost* inaudible gasp, from where Mahtab had exited the room.

Sadie became incessant, "I want my father. I want us to go home. Until then, there's no 'understanding' between us!"

Akbar had lost interest in her petulance. He stood and slowly walked to the door, then in a self-satisfied tone of voice, asked, "You say that you want your father? You think he is waiting to take you home now? Huh!" He toyed with her emotions like a cat with a mouse as he kept dangling out questions, "Who do you think brought you here? Who do you think delivered you...to *me*? Who do you think sent me in here, this delightful morning?" He ran his fingers through his thick beard, scratched his chin, then with an evil grin purred, "Well now, let's find out together, shall we?" He opened the door and called down the corridor, "Jack...

Oh, Ja-ack, you're on, someone wants her *father*!"

Akbar relished at what was about to unravel in his presence.

## Chapter Eleven

Jack "Cannibal" Jones, slid into the room, sweat dripping
from his brow and staining the collar of his captain's uniform
in which he had slept, off and on, the night before. Once
inside, he gestured for Akbar to leave. It wasn't until Jack
threw in an adamant, "Get out," with a nod pointing to the
door before Akbar reluctantly departed the room.

Jack closed and bolted the door as a yelp of pure joy and
relief came thrusting at him with the full force and energy of
his daughter's embrace, "Daddy, Dad! It's you, it's really
you. I'm so relieved to see you!" Sadie grabbed ahold, tightly
and began sobbing like a lost child. "Oh, thank God you're
here! Now we can leave! Let's get out of here, Dad! Let's
go!"

She finally relinquished her tight hold on fear as her father's presence gave her some sense of security and direction. "Dad, what is going on? I've been so scared! What are we doing here? Did they grab you up, like they did me? Were you on the plane? Did they make you fly it, Dad?" She paused long enough for a breath, then went at it again, envisioning the fierce firestorm that had engulfed their home, "Oh God, our house...the fire...it was terrible, it was enormous and relentless! Did you see it? Weren't you home Dad? How did you get out?!" Sadie pulled away from their embrace to look at her father's face, wondering why there had been no response...to *any* of her questions. Again, she prompts a question, this one, she would make certain he would answer, "Dad? Can we go now? Can we go home?"

Jack peeled Sadie's arms from around his waist and walked her back to a chair. He seemed agitated with all the probing, as he sat her down; putting her in her place. Then, standing behind her, his hands on her shoulders as if to hold her there, he began to answer her questions, the ones he deemed necessary.

"Sadie, there is nothing left for us back in Virginia. The fire took everything." He paused for a split second, then delivered the next of many punches, "We are here for the foreseeable future. We have a mission, with duties that must be fulfilled; right here, in this country. It is where we must be. This is home now." With his hands holding her down, he felt the tautness building within her body as she twitched and flinched her shoulders to release the tension, and his hold.

She turned in her seat and sharply asked, "What are you saying? We're not leaving?" Sadie's confusion inflamed her next words, "How can you be so willing to give up our home; everything we have known? For *this place?*" She threw herself back into the seat while making wild suggestions, "We can just drive back to the airport, and, and...Get back on the plane. You can just fly us home on that thing. Whose plane is that anyway? Can we take it? You flew it in, right? Right Dad? Dad?? Jack!?"

Jack heard the tenor of mistrust rising in her voice. "Jack is it, huh?" He released a big sigh as he continued, "Calm down Sadie. You are going to be alright. Everything is under control. We are safe here, on these grounds. But, we aren't going anywhere. Can you live with that?"

She shifted nervously in the seat as she thought to herself, *his demeaner is different...harsh...cold.* Then just as coldly, Sadie stated, "I don't know what to make of all this." While silently compiling a mental list of the questions left to be answered, and the flood of new ones forming rapidly.

Jack cracked his knuckles as he went on, "This isn't easy--for any of us." The coward in him stayed standing behind her, hidden, so he did not have to look her in the eyes for the next blow, "All you have to do is just what is asked of you, and above all, trust me."

He started pacing behind her, "You know Ali and I go way back, right?"

Sadie turned in her seat again and answered slowly and even more confused at the sudden change of topic, "Yes, of course."

"You obviously don't know the details of Ali's and my history, but you understand enough to be clear that what I'm about to tell you is damn serious, not to be taken lightly, and frankly, not a request." Jack began to take full command as he walked around, in front of Sadie's seat. "Do you understand what I'm telling you here?"

She looked to her father with deepened concern, "Yes, I know of the missions you two used to run; 'Top Secret' stuff, 'Classified.' You never spoke of it. I learned more from reading the Military News than from either of you. But I've always trusted you Dad, you're the only family I have; you, and Ali."

Sadie's senses become heightened, "You have never given me a reason to not trust you…Jack. You can tell me anything, what is it?"

Jack still would not look at her as he returned to pacing, now in front of her. He mentally refocused on the long decertation he had been practicing for months, hell, years, really. He began, rather dramatically, "The world we live in is a very dangerous place. There are international terrorists, treasonous gangsters within governments and even pirates on the high seas, all infiltrating through third world regimes into the very fabric of our flag and our way of life."

Sadie leaned forward in her chair, listening intently.

Her father adhered to the tone and cadence of his well-rehearsed speech, "Some time ago, we were informed of a plot, a horrific one, against the world. One that would unleash evil upon the entire world at *once*! Unless…we were to step in and take hold of the situation."

Sadie questioned, "Isn't that what you do every single day? You, our military, you all stop evil, all over the world, right? Isn't that what you and Ali do? Every, single, day??"

The room suddenly darkened. A cloud had crossed into the sunlight, that had been shining from the aperture above the tower dome, where they sat. Slowly a chill encircled Sadie. Every hair on the back of her neck stood at attention as Jack filled in more details.

"Like I said, evil is upon us and all good people are called to action, and we must do our part."

The chill enters Sadie and grabs a hold of her heart as she fears the worst for her father, "Dad, what do you have to do? Is it dangerous? More dangerous than anything you've done before? Will Ali and his team be with you?"

Jack rolled his eyes and looked down at her innocence, before releasing a smug huff under his breath. He walked slowly in front of her, put his hands on the arms of her chair and got right in her face, "Not me honey, *you*!" He stood upright again and poured it on thick, "Your country…no, all the people of the world need *you* to do your part to ensure that evil does not entwine itself into our world."

Sadie bolts out of the chair. Her shock sharpened and informed her tone and her wits, "Me? What the hell, Dad? Are you serious; what am I supposed to do…what *could* I do? I have no training, I'm not a soldier, I don't know anything about secret missions or Special Forces! There must be a hundred others, in the military, that could do this mission, whatever it is; why me?"

Just then her heart flickered, like the flame of a candle blowing in the wind. The tension continued to rise between them as she realized that her father was not going to fix this nightmare for her; he was climbing right into it!

"I know it is hard for you to take this all in. We didn't have much time to plan for this," he lied, knowing this plan was in place for the better part of twenty years. "*They* needed to have someone they could trust. *They* turned to me because of my extensive knowledge and multiple tours in the Persian

Gulf. And our personal situation at home, you know, that it

is just you and me, no one else. For once it helped that you

didn't really have any friends, being home-schooled, and all.

The fewer contact points the better, you know how it is.

Plus, they have known my work for decades. They know

that we, you and I, would be able to do this…'for the

people'." He hammed it up, again.

"They need someone with courage and smarts who can

quickly execute the duties for the mission to be a success. It

is you, Sadie. You are the only one we can trust at this time.

If there was a different way, I would have pushed for it, but

there isn't. Trust me."

He began selling it to her hard, "This is an honor to be

chosen. We are dealing with some highly classified stuff

here, Sadie. You are a known entity to them Sadie, they are

well-aware that you are the daughter of a soldier with top-

secret clearance, and you will do what is expected of you."

He finally came over to her and grabbed her hand, as a father might, "You will be safe and you will be protected, at all times. I promise." He lied, again.

"Sooooo, what do we need to do exactly? Or I should say, what do I need to do?"

Jack continued, confident that all he had to do was bring it home.

"The 'powers that be' have arranged for a young man to be named the King of Iran. He comes from the lineage of the old guard that had been installed into power decades ago. He is the son of the old King, a friend of the West--one of us. He will be placed into power again, to rule this country and take control of its people."

Sadie is shaking her head no, as if that could change what she was hearing, "But, why?"

"Aren't you listening, Sadie? In order to 'save our world'."

"I still don't get it, what do they want from me?  What am I supposed to do?"

Jack kept up the speech, line for line, "There may be resistance from the villagers and shepherds from the countryside.  We know Tehran, with its westernized culture wants this to happen; they are begging for it.  But we will have some resistance from the peasants who haven't yet been exposed to all our great technological advances."

"Ok, but…Where do I come in?"

"Sadie, dear.  We, um, we will need you to act as his queen."  He glanced over for a response but didn't wait for one, "You are to be wed, in an arranged marriage, to the new King of Iran; like I said, it is actually quite an honor and…"

Sadie looked at her father like she didn't recognize him, "Whoa, wait a minute.  Marriage? 'Arranged' at that?  Me?...Who would believe it?...I don't.  This is insane." Sadie is finding it all too incredulous. "We're in Iran. Persia. The old country. This has nothing to do with me, with us!  Why are we *installing* any power here; let alone a King…and me!? These people have survived thousands of years without our help, what are we *really* doing here? This is crazy!"

Looking around in disbelief, she noticed the light brighten once again through the aperture above the dome. Dust particles shimmered and moved in a coalescing dance in the beam of light as if trying to bring peace to her frenzied thoughts and emotions. The sight beckoned her attention.

Then Jack interrupted the fleeting moment, "This won't be for long. Think of it as a cultural studies course or a long vacation in an exotic land. You will have handlers—er, body guards—with you at all times, so you won't have to worry about your safety one bit."

He eased up, "The people need to see a soft feminine touch; a kind face, someone in which they can place their complete trust and confidence. You will be perfect!"

Jack, now believing she understands the predicament, fills in a few more details, "You just need to soak in some local color, pick up a few phrases in Farsi, study a few of their old traditions.  In no time you will win over their hearts and minds; then, before you know it, this will all be over…in a few months."

"*A few months*?!" Sadie repeated, aghast.

Chapter Twelve

Fort Bragg, North Carolina, USA

Twilight ushered in the black sedan as it completed the five-hour journey from Dulles to Fort Bragg. It entered the east gate, cleared security, and headed to the airfield hangars, with purpose.

Ali exited the vehicle to enter the voluminous hanger. Once inside, he headed past a military transport jet that was feverishly being loaded and two helicopters that were fully armed and at the ready. Ali walked briskly toward the back corner where a few benches were positioned around a desk and two huge white-boards.

He called out to his team while in mid-step, "Yo, get in here." The men were just finishing the final checklist for the weapons and equipment they had been loading into the aircraft. As they exited the plane and gathered around Ali, he inquired, "Where's McCord? Is 'Sticks' back yet?

Sanchez spoke up, "He called just a minute ago, he should be pulling up to the hangar."

Just then, Jason "Sticks" McCord double-timed it through the side door of the structure. He was humping in with his duffle and several weapons cases. He was laser-focused and mission-ready. Nothing was going keep him from bringing this one home to completion.

"Glad you could join us," Miller chimed in, watching McCord methodically load his gear into the aircraft and secure it.

Immediately, the order came from Ali, "Green-light, we're at 'go'; let's move out." Ali was not messing around; he was leading his elite team of trained Special Forces to the next phase of the mission.

Chapter Thirteen

Altitude: 45,000 feet, somewhere over the Atlantic

"All right, let's wrap this up," Ali wanted a recap before

landing at their clandestine destination. "Stevens, want to do

the honors? Give it to us, clean and sweet."

Stevens was stoic, but with a sense of humor that helped

during these long flights. He fired right up in his sweet,

southern drawl, "Well, let's see now. Looks like we've got

ourselves a group of elite bastards that have infiltrated *our*

government, and they ain't playing nice with the rest of the

world, either. Worse than that, they've bought off some of

our own, who have forgotten their oath to the greatest

document ever written for mankind—the US Constitution—

next to the Holy Bible, that is." He shook his head with

disappointment, "How could our brothers and sisters in arms, forsake their Title 10 Oath, to protect and preserve the Constitution for the United States…the last stand between freedom and tyranny!"

He took off his cap, wiped his brow and then went back to his performance, "Here it is in a nutshell, these elites want to take over the world, but us boys—*Thee United States Military*— we're frowning on that. So, these elites plan on picking a fight; one that could be 'biblical' in size and devastation. Yup, these high-dollar, shit-for-brains are looking to start a war, Armageddon-style, 'between the king of the west and the king of the east;' which, oh, by the way, the elite bastards own both sides of this impending war. Then, get this, here's where *our* dirty government comes in, they toss us, freedom-fightin'-Americans, into the brawl, to 'come to the rescue', and before ya know it…they've created the mother of all false flags…WORLD WAR 3! During the fog of war, and after they've slaughtered enough of us poor folk, they plan on putting into operation, a global slave system, the likes of which this world ain't seen yet! Like that book, 1984, only this new crap is real, and powered by their god--A.I.! Now, I ask ya, why would anyone in their right mind want something called *Artificial* Intelligence controlling every single aspect of their life?" He stopped for a second then sarcastically added, "It's been working so well for the commies, ain't it? So they thought they'd do it everywhere!" He looked away, then came back with a definitive, "Dumb bastards!"

Ali, chuckled under his breath at the performance, then relieved the men for the night, "Alright. Alright...we've been up for a solid 36. Everyone, turn in, the sun is breaking the horizon. We'll have time to hit it again before we land, which looks like another nine hours to go."

Jason "Sticks" McCord looked out the window at the rising light with resolve, as his memory wrapped around his favorite girl.

## Chapter Fourteen


## Palace Grounds, Yazd, Iran


Sadie had become accustomed to taking a morning walk in the palace gardens over the past several weeks. The garden had become a sanctuary of peace. Each morning she strolled the length of the magnificent, rectangular, reflecting pool that was centered between rows of fruit trees growing inside the perimeter of the high walls.

Of course, she was not alone, never was. Her handlers—security, were always lurking nearby. She would try to ignore them, or sometimes even, irritate them, by purposely dawdling in the garden; 'contemplating…things.'

Today, she sat by the pool's edge and thought of the events of yesterday; recollecting each moment, before trying to erase it from her psyche, but the images came flooding in, one by one: The soon-to-be-king had entered her suite, with her father and the vile one in tow. There was an introduction, which was as cold and impersonal as his handshake. Then, in a most unceremonious manner, he foisted the "engagement" ring upon her finger, making it "official."

He had played his role, and claimed his prize, just as he had been directed.

All Sadie could think of, during the horrid instant that the ring was being jammed onto her finger, was *It's too tight, it's too damn tight! Get it off of me!* But the words could not escape, and neither could she.

She shuddered the memory off.

As she sat by the pool, she dipped her hand into the coolness of the water, and reflected farther back in time. The water was soothing as she contemplated the potential, she had hoped, for her life… A life that had only recently started to become interesting, and good; fun even, as she revisited her last few months back home through her mind's eye. *That young girl in Vienna, Virginia, visiting the record shop each week, in search of music and finding a note, a love note.* Just then the image of Jason, playing his air drums, flickered into her recollection, then faded away as the ring of engagement cut into her flesh.

Her awareness came rushing back into the present as she looked at the golden bauble, this time in the sunlight, and confirmed aloud, "It's too tight, and damn gaudy too!" Looking at the ring, and her life, now with abhorrence!

Her tension was palpable from attempting to contain her rage. Over the past weeks, her anger was silenced into depression, as helplessness took up permanent residence in her mind. She tried to evict the feeling, but she had lost all hope with the recent actions of her father—*no…Jack…Jack "Cannibal" Jones*—she corrected her own thought; then gazed into the reflective pool for a way out.

Sadie watched the bright white, orange and golden koi entwine together as they fought for their morning meal. It was mesmerizing, like watching the flame of a fire being stoked. Their fish tails rippled the waters; making the Sun's rays dance upon the pool. The Light made her smile, if only for a moment.

Then the heat set in; her morning stroll had breached high-noon. The intensity of the bright sun, was getting intolerable. She glanced to see if the "lurkers" were still following her every move. Of course, they were. She apathetically headed back to her palatial suite, seeking the darkened space, that was now called home.

Chapter Fifteen


Palace Suite, Yazd, Iran

Several months later


Mahtab had become a trusted friend and companion to Sadie over the last several months.  She continued to help Sadie execute each task demanded of her; everything from lessons in Farsi, cultural history, Persian etiquette, to studies in fine art and ancient poetry, just to name a few.

After only months of study, Sadie was astonished by her own grasp of the teachings, "I don't know how or why I pickup this stuff so quickly, as if I already had possession of the knowledge and I just needed to polish up on it or something--*or maybe*--" She stopped to laugh, "I was *really* a Persian Princess in a prior life!"

Mahtab's eyes flickered with the light of hope that those words carried.

Sadie saw her glee, "I was only kidding, Mahtab. You gotta let me blow off steam every now and then; even if it is with a silly joke." Sadie pushed herself away from the plate of food that had been brought in while they had been chatting. "I can't take much more of this," she admitted with a tone of defeat she had not recognized in herself before.

Mahtab looked at her dear friend, with concern. The many hours, day in and day out, that were demanded of Sadie had taken a toll on her mind and her body. She had become incredibly thin and frail from it all. "My dear, do not let the cold wind blow out your light."

Sadie looked at her, a little confused, but she got the gist of what Mahtab was saying.

"Please finish your dinner, another bite of kabob or a small piece of lavash with some yogurt, you will love it, oh it is so delicious," Mahtab coaxed, "After you eat, I have a surprise for you!"

Sadie smiled then softly stated, "*You,* my friend, bring light into my world; a world where I only see darkness."

Sadie's days had been packed with tutors and studies, being pushed, and pulled in every direction at everyone else's beck-and-call. Her only respite came during the evenings, when she and Mahtab could sit together, play backgammon, sip tea, and share stories from past and present, never delving too far into what the future held...before tonight!

Heading back to the table, Sadie glanced at the food; she was uninterested, "I'll eat later." But her mood perked up a little when she saw the playful glimmer in Mahtab's eyes, "Tell me more about this surprise!"

Mahtab reached deep into the pocket of her very, poofy, full-length skirt and pulled out a small, metal box, which she held tightly, close to her chest, as she waddled over to the center of the room. Once atop the crimson and gold rug, she plopped herself down, and let her veil slide down her back to the floor; she reveled in the freedom she could now express in Sadie's presence. With glee and mischief, she gestured to Sadie to come over; patting the rug with her hand, "Come, I have something to show you."

Sadie was already heading her way, curiously asking, "What are you up to now, Mahtab?"

Mahtab giggled while lifting the metal box up toward Sadie's face, who was now standing next to her, so she can see the mystic box for herself. Mahtab teased, "See this? It belongs to my grandmother," she said, as she opened the small box and tipped the contents onto the rug.

Sadie laughed. "Playing cards? That's my big surprise?" She looked at Mahtab with amused wonder as she sat on the rug, across from her friend. "Ok, what do you want to play?"

Mahtab, began sorting the cards, pulling out some of them to set them aside then shuffling the remaining ones together as she knowingly smiled, "Not *playing* cards, these are *truth*-tellers, they tell your fortune!"

"You mean they tell my *future*?" Sadie's expression sank with disappointment. She then responded before getting an answer, "I don't want to know. I've already been *advised* as to what's in store for me!" She stood up, walked over to her bed, and flopped into it; giving up any hope for her future.

"Come here," Mahtab beckoned as she fanned the selected cards in her hand to view each one; they had been used so many times, they were torn and tattered, some faded into oblivion. She indulged in one final shuffle, with the performance of a Las Vegas dealer; this part of the fortune telling she had managed to master. "Come. You must make a wish and cut the cards." She kept looking at Sadie; playfully teasing her to return to the floor where the cards were now placed in a neat, tight stack. "Good, you come back…sit, make a wish…a good one…and keep it for yourself, don't tell me, not a word," Mahtab's accent was thick, but her English had become proficient.

Sadie gave in, mostly because Mahtab was so excited to play fortune teller. She sat on the floor and put her hand on the deck, "Ok, O – K," Sadie looked up as if searching for that one 'good' wish. "Nothing…nothing comes to mind," she sighs, twirling the once tight engagement ring freely on her finger. She had lost so much weight from all the stress that now she could barely keep the ring on her hand. "Hmmm, I can't think of anything…" she said, tapping her fingers rhythmically on the cards just before the damn ring fell onto the stack. "Yup, that's it! I got it!" She decisively cut the deck and said, "So when will it come true?"

"Nuh-ah, first I must *tell*, then it come true!" Mahtab got comfortable, closed her eyes, took a long, deep, cleansing breath, then, as if entering a trance, she was ready to begin the fortune.

Silence.

Nothing.

Sadie laughed out loud; she couldn't help it.

Mahtab opened one eye, looked around, then opened the other and blurted out, "Ok, maybe I cannot read fortune, I never know what card goes where. But, tomorrow, we go to the bazaar—to find a real fortune teller. Tomorrow, we find the truth!"

Sadie shakes her head at the antics, "Oh Mahtab, you're too much. Besides, what do you mean 'go to the bazaar'? With *these* goons watching over me?"

"What is this goon you speak of?"

Sadie smiled again, rolled her eyes, and reminded Mahtab, "My security goons, er, guards…my security guards. They will never let me go to the bazaar."

"It's ok, I do everything. I know how to arrange. I know Reza's mother. She will help. We will go to bazaar, it will be good for you, and the goons eh, guards. It is time you go into the peoples. They need to see you and you need to meet the peoples you will soon be guiding."

Sadie was taken aback, "People I willing be guiding? No, no that's not in the script. I'm just here for the fake wedding as a fake queen…nothing to see here. Think of me as a prop; a very pissed-off prop."

Unbelieving in that line of thinking Mahtab sounds off, "Pshhh, you have much to learn. Tomorrow your *real* school begins!"

Chapter Sixteen

Isfahan, Iran

The Grand Bazaar

The drive from Yazd to Isfahan was long, but surprisingly quick, when done in the wee hours of the morning.

Mahtab had made good on her word to 'arrange it' so Sadie could visit the Grand Bazaar of Isfahan.  On the drive over she would share little details of the ancient grounds, "This is the oldest Persian bazaar, I think.  It is a big one too; maybe the biggest market in the Middle East.  Some of the shops have the same type of thing for sale for over 400 years!"  Her eyes widened in her own amazement.

Sadie was more impressed by Mahtab's accomplishment of having Reza and a driver be the only security for her and her friend on this newest of adventures. She had to ask, "Mahtab, I must know, how did you do it? How did you get Reza to agree to this? Leaving the grounds without my usual security detail and coming—of all places—to the bazaar!"

Mahtab's hijab was tightly secured around her face, as was Sadie's, now that they were out in public again. Only her full, round face poked through the veil as her signature smile gave way to her spirited Persian accent, "It was easy. I use my head. I say, look, if you bring her with limousine and many guards to protect her, then people will think, maybe she is someone we must see, maybe bother her, or take her, she must be very special, maybe even valuable. But, if you go like you are nobody, then nobody will care about you."

Reza chimed in, "I must admit, it was simple, but brilliant." Then he told the driver, "Ok, stop here, we will walk in the rest of the way, you pull up, close to the gates, and wait for us there."

The driver did exactly as directed, as Reza checked his weapons, tucked them under his shirt and covered them up to make sure they were not visible. He readied himself to discreetly escort Sadie through the labyrinth of shops. Looking around the vehicle, he unlocked the car door, and as it was opening, he quietly exhaled, "Why did I agree to this?"

Sadie clutched her veil tighter around her head and face with one hand as she began pointing with the other at some of the most beautiful architectural features she had seen. The ancient designs were a tapestry of delight for the eyes.

Reza stood close, behind the ladies, careful to not touch them, certainly not in view of the Iranian Revolutionary Guard that patrolled the streets. He moved into position, close behind them, watching everything from, an arm's length away. "Ladies, I implore you, stay together, stay close to me at all times, and please, whatever you do, don't stray off into any shops by yourself. We have one hour." He stopped to sternly make his point in Farsi, "Mahtab, look at me…one hour, *YEK JAM*, not any longer." He was very familiar with Mahtab's playful nature and wanted to stave it off, this time. "One hour. If we get in and out during the morning hours the crowds will be less, our exposure will be less, yet you can get whatever it was you needed that was so critical for the ceremony tomorrow."

Sadie's stomach turned at those words, as she thought to herself, *the bloody wedding…it's time has come… already! Tomorrow, I'll have to play out my wedding day, with a man I don't know, or even care to know.*

Mahtab was grumbling under her breath, but loud enough for Reza to hear, "One hour, one hour? How can I do everything in one hour!" Then she grabbed Sadie's hand the moment they entered through the Qeysarie Gate, the main entrance to the Grand Bazaar. She didn't run, she walked, as Reza requested, but she walked at triple speed; determined to find the fortune teller's booth. She turned and whispered to Sadie, "This is a great place to get lost, then find your way home," as she pulled Sadie along by the hand.

Into the maze they went, scurrying through the growing crowds, this way and that, with Reza chasing along for the wild ride. Mahtab was on a mission to find the fortune teller as they whirled by shops of every kind. There were shops for metal work, jewelry, paintings, and clothes. At a turn here, the scent of fragrant spices filled the air, a turn there and stacks of hand painted fabrics flashed their vivid colors of Autumn leaves. Down one alley were rows of hand-woven carpets, some made of silk, some made of wool; down the next even more beauty could be found in the most unexpected places as they delved into the intricate network of bustling alleys.

Sadie was in awe as she sensed something exquisite in every direction, slowing her pace to look up at the architecture of the intricate ivory-colored, dome above, then rushing through archways of masterfully laid nature scenes in mosaics of turquoise and blues, smelling the essence of Bergamot in the brewing of morning tea, witnessing the gathering crowd tending to their daily needs as the clanking of merchants and music filled the sound waves. It was an amazing place, throbbing with the colors of life!

Down one more alley, before Mahtab finally slowed the pace, but continued her search. "It should be here." She walked past a few more store fronts and turned the corner; still with a tight grip of Sadie's hand.

She stopped in the middle of the alley suddenly, and slowly looked around. An eerie light found its way from the slender, snake-like panes of glass atop the ceiling of one distinct alleyway. Halfway down the row, the light dimmed. Mahtab could barely make out the sign, but with a squeal of exuberance she began her high-speed chatter, "It's here. It's here! I got it. Ok, we go in. Reza-jun we see you in eh, thirty minutes?" Mahtab tried to hurry Sadie into the fortune teller's shop, without having Reza join them; imagining, if only for a second, that Reza would let that happen.

"Ever the jokester, Mahtab...What are you suggesting?" Reza moved into position, blocking the alley between the entrance and the interior of the shop where Sadie now stood. He tried to provide as much protection from view as possible. Checking the surroundings, he stated, "Not a chance, I'm staying right here. I'm not letting her out of my sight," he huffed, as if he thought Mahtab had lost her mind. "You've got 10 minutes ladies. Then we need to make our way back." He was very matter-of-fact as he stood guard, in front of the shop, while Mahtab made their presence known to the absent fortune teller.

"Sahlam? Yoo-hoo? Sahlaaaam?" Mahtab called out, impatiently, fully aware this was cutting into her 'ten minutes'.

A rather old woman, peered from behind a thick purple curtain. She appeared a little annoyed. Her eyes squinted, looking at those who had interrupted her breakfast. as she brushed a few crumbs of pita and feta that had caught themselves between her straggling, gray, chin hairs.

Mahtab stated in Farsi that they needed a fortune told, just one, looking toward Sadie, and asked if she would do it, now, and do it quickly.

The woman came out of the shadow and stood for a while, not saying a word. She walked closer to Sadie, looked her over, from bottom to top, then shook her head 'no' as she sat down in her official fortune teller's seat.

Mahtab took a step forward and before she could object, the woman defiantly stated in Farsi, "I cannot read her; her Light is too bright! You must leave, now!"

Sadie felt a rush of air swirl about the length of her entire body. It lifted her veil as several onlookers stole a glimpse of her. The desert eddy became emboldened as it pushed Sadie and Reza, out the door and into the alley.

"Leave now, run!" the fortune yelled, in English, behind them.

The alley was buzzing with people; the chatter amongst them reverberated through the crowd. This one whispered to that one; that one told two more, until a mass of people had gathered around Sadie in no time.

Reza was single-minded in getting her into the vehicle and out of this growing danger. He had no choice, he grabbed her hand through the veil, as he pushed through the crowd. Sadie felt that same rush of energy as when they rushed through the airport, in what seemed like a lifetime ago.

They picked up speed, but so did the crowd. It was like a game of Pong, as she bounced off people getting closer to see if the rumors could be true. All the jostling was pulling on her veil. Slowly she could feel the damn thing slipping down her hair; exposing the forbidden.

Reza shouted out to the ladies, "I see the car, we are almost there. Can you keep up this pace?"

Sadie looked up to answer him as the veil threatened full exposure. She tried to use her free hand to pull the fabric into place and just then...*ta-ting-ting-ting*. "Stop!!" She shrieked. "Stop Reza!! I just lost the ring!!" She frantically yells, "It just slipped off my finger! It has to be right here, it just happened! I felt it slip away as I reached for my veil." Sadie was desperately searching the ground; as much as she hated the ugly ring, she was to be wed with it...tomorrow!

Just a few feet away, a glimmer catches sunlight. "There! There it is!" She pushed through the crowd to get to the ring, but before she could reach it, she saw the hand of a young boy, no more than ten years old, grab the golden treasure and run down an alley. Without thinking she yells out, "Get that kid! He's running away with the ring!"

Reza was angry, but one would never know it. His focus was on Sadie's safety as he commanded, "We are heading to car, right now! I'll get the ring once you're secure! Let's go!" He rushed the two ladies toward the waiting car.

As they were running, Sadie could hear the calls again. The chatter of the crowd had once again turned to a mulled chant, "Attisheh ma, Attisheh ma."

They finally reached the car; Reza was about to open the door to secure Sadie into the vehicle, when an old man appeared, as if from nowhere, right amongst the three of them. He thrust out his fist toward Sadie. Reza grabbed the man's wrist, reflexively, and was about to put him down to the ground, in one sweeping move.

But the old man quickly opened his fist, and said, "It is yours! This is for you! Take it!" Looking at Sadie, he exclaimed, "It is your destiny!"

Sadie, Reza and Mahtab all looked into his open hand at the same time. There, wrapped in a torn and tattered parchment, between the elder's wrinkled fingers, laid the ring!

Sadie quickly grabbed the bundle while looking into the man's eyes. They were warm and kind, like the eyes of a wise old grandfather, might be. She thanked him before feeling Mahtab pulling at her clothes, from inside the car.

Reza hurriedly secured the ladies into the vehicle then got in himself, telling the driver, "Move out, let's get out of here." The vehicle slowly made its way through the crowd, as Reza thought to himself, *another adventure, brought to you by my little family-friend, Mahtab, comes to a nail-biting close.* He finally exhaled when the car cleared through the crowd.

As the vehicle passed the old man, the elder nodded to Sadie, knowingly, and once again called out, "It is your destiny!"

Sadie slid the ring back onto her finger, afraid of what could have happened to her, to Reza, and even Mahtab had the ring not been found. She made a fist, so it could not escape her finger again. Then stuffed the wrapper into her pocket. She looked at the ring and shook her head, as the old man's words rippled through her mind, then whispered, "I came for a fortune and got *this* as my destiny."

The chanting of the people began to wane, but she could still hear in the distance, "Attisheh ma. Attisheh ma. Attisheh ma."

Chapter Seventeen

Reza returned Sadie, safely, to her palace suite. "It is late, ladies. Tomorrow is a very big day; you will need your rest." He closed the door, while Mahtab continued her chatter with Sadie. "Boy, that woman can talk," he said to the guards as he smiled at Mahtab's zest and stamina with the spoken word.

Mahtab and Sadie walked deeper into the suite where they saw two women putting the final touches on what would become Sadie's wedding gown. They had the lavish dress hanging from a mannequin in the center of the room, with its long train wrapped at its feet like a coiled snake. All the trappings for this ceremony were laid upon several glass carts, on either side of the dress. No detail was left out;

Sadie had everything one could imagine, from the soles of her satin shoes to the crown of her golden tiara; it was a wedding fit for a queen. The incredible extravagances strewn at her finger tips were awe-inspiring.

Mahtab walked over and carefully picked up the solid gold tiara with both hands, and turned to place it on Sadie's head. "You will be the most treasured queen our land has known. Your Light outshines the brilliance of gold."

Sadie felt the weight of the tiara, in more ways than one. She peeled it off her head and tossed it, back onto the cart. Brooding, she sighed, "I'm really tired, Mahtab. We can play dress up tomorrow, huh? Sorry. I just need some time to myself."

Her dark, somber reality, was painted on the facade of wedding-white fabric, hanging from the mannequin, in front of her. She looked at the dress. Hopeless, she searched for a ray of light; silently wondering, at this final hour, *is there a way out of this darkness?*

Mahtab chimed in, "Yes, of course. We let you sleep. Everyone out. Quickly…Zoodbash, zoodbash!" Mahtab commanded the women in Farsi to quickly depart the palace suite. Leaving Sadie, alone, with her thoughts.

Exhausted, Sadie headed to bed. While undressing, she emptied her pockets and threw the contents onto the table next to her bed as she changed into her sleeping gown. She walked into the bathroom and stood at the basin, looking into the mirror for a long time. The image gazed back, without any expression. She waited for an answer to her silent inquiry. It did not come.

She brushed her teeth, brushed her hair and for this last night, she brushed away the possibility of the past several months just being a nightmare, from which she could have awakened.

She walked back into the suite; with a deep sigh she climbed into bed, leaned across the copper table to blow out the oil lamp that cast its warm glow into the darkness. It flickered in her soft breath, but did not go out. Just then, the tattered paper, in which the old man had wrapped the ring, caught a glimmer of the flickering light. She sat up to retrieve the crumpled paper. Flattened it out and held it up to the light.

"What the…? How can this be? How did that old man know of my birthmark, and to draw it, in such detail?!" She lifts the hem of her nightgown to reveal the birthmark on her upper thigh, the one she had mocked and hidden all her life. She compared the exactness of the gold-leafed symbol on the paper, to the mark on her inner thigh. She tilted the paper from one side to the other, attempting to make out the scrawl of lettering beneath the symbol. Moving in closer, to reflect the Light, the message became illuminated, as Sadie read the words aloud, "It is your destiny!"

Chapter Eighteen


Becoming A Bride


"Ughhhh…Turn off the lights," Sadie moaned, from the middle of a tousled heap of bedsheets surrounding her brief night of sleep. She had spent most of the prior night and into the wee hours, contemplating, crying, begging, praying for a last-minute savior to come to her rescue. Yet, here she was—alone—on the darkest day of her life; except for that unrelenting beam penetrating her slumber!

"Ah, come on, get that light out of my face," she said, reluctant to rise. "Ok…I'm up, I'm up already," she grumbled as she lay amidst the mess of bedding, she had been wrestling in her sleep. She rubbed her eyes, expecting to find one of the palace women standing next to her, with a giant lamp, trying to awaken her, but that was not so.

The intruder was a solitary ray of morning sunlight, reflecting itself from the facets of the golden crown Sadie had tossed upon the cart the night before. It beamed directly onto Sadie as she wriggled to avoid its brightness. The light was persistent in making its presence known.

Lifting her head, she managed to move out of its path before taking a slow, long, view of her surroundings. Then, with a deep breath of acquiescence, she exhaled, "Well, I guess it's time to get up and become the 'blushing bride-to-be'; my final duty to fulfill." She looked up to the heavens as if asking for help, one last time; before dropping her head in submission. Then she heard her own voice aloud, dripping with the truth, and a heap of sarcasm, "Yeah, time to get dolled up for the alter--you're about to be sacrificed."

Before she could get out of bed, several women quietly entered her suite. They had patiently waited for Sadie to arise as they methodically began the wedding-day rituals. She was fed a light breakfast, bathed, gently massaged and pampered, then had a soft dusting of makeup applied, before being passed to the royal hair dressers who proceeded to twist and bind her long, chestnut locks, into a lavish beehive, fit for a Persian Queen. Just in time to deliver her back to the teams of women, working their wedding wonder, who were ready to dress the bride in preparation for the public procession and evening nuptial.

Sadie had spent the entire day allowing herself to be molded into the queen-bride. There she stood, draped in a silk robe, in front of a semi-circle of seven, full-length, mirrors, that had been rolled to the center of the room. Beside her stood the mannequin, displaying the wedding gown that would soon be bound to her body. Sadie watched the images of herself reflecting from the various mirrors, as the ladies began to dress her. Slowly, each layer of the ceremonial dress was meticulously placed into position upon her. With each layer, Sadie lost more of herself. Once the last ribbon had cinched the dress tightly around Sadie's delicate neck, she looked into the seven mirrors once again. Her eyes moved from one mirror to the next, before she asked herself, *Who are you? Every, single, thing, that made you, 'Sadie Jones' has been stripped away. I don't even recognize you!* She was about to cry for herself, but even her tears betrayed her.

Just then Mahtab burst into the room, eager to see the ladies' artistry in creating the royal bride. She slowed her walk; in awe of the beauty she was witnessing. Mahtab encircled Sadie, and then motioned for the tiara from the hands of the hairdresser, "Oh please, allow me to crown our bride." She gleamed, while stepping back to view the perfect placement for the golden headdress. Instead, what she saw, was the emptiness within her friend's eyes; as tears then filled her own.

Mahtab recognized the look of anguish as she lovingly placed her hand on Sadie's cheek to hearten her, before softly whispering to Sadie, "Oh my dear princess, without darkness, there can be no light."

The tears spilled from Mahtab's eyes as she gently placed the golden crown atop Sadie's head and solemnly stated, "Attisheh ma, the Light of our light. Attisheh ma."

The women had rolled in an eighth mirror and aligned it behind the bride, so she could get a full-circle view of herself.

Mahtab slowly turned Sadie toward the full-length looking glass before stepping away, to allow the bride space to see her dominion.

Surrendering, Sadie lifted her gaze from the floor to the mirror before her. She viewed the many reflections of herself; seven fractured images behind her, and one, complete lie, dressed in white, lay ahead. She feigned a smile to complete the lie, as she stood in front of the mirror

for what seemed like a lifetime.

# Chapter Nineteen

## The Wedding

The people were gathering, filling the streets and alleys. Some came to smell the beautiful floral arrangements that cascaded from the rooftops to the street lamps. Some came to hear the music and listen to the sacred poetry being recited from the call tower. Some came to watch the procession of royals before the wedding. And some came because they had heard the rumor from the Persian bazaar and needed to see her with their own eyes.

They came from all walks of life to witness this event; all wanting to capture a glimpse of the beautiful bride who would soon become the queen—*their* queen. Their admiration was pulsating with the growing crowd as they pushed in, closer and closer, tightening their circle around the Palace grounds.

Deep inside the stone walls, in the main security bunker, Reza paced back and forth. He was worried, but adamant in his statements to the teams in charge of securing the event, "There's no way we can support a motorcade escort on the outer streets and into that crowd. People have come in from Tehran and even farther; these are not just our local neighbors and farmers, these are strangers. We have no idea who is in that crowd. Those are not our villagers, nor our friends carrying those damn signs. Did you read some of those threats? It's too dangerous, the crowd is way bigger than we had planned, or imagined, so we have cancelled the processional drive, but..."

He wiped the sweat from his brow into his sleeve, "*Captain* Jack maintains he wants a procession of some kind, so he is having a crew extend the stage for the wedding and making a runway, for them to walk through the crowd. I fought him, but he wouldn't budge. So, we must work with what we *can* control. Let's keep their exposure as tight as possible while they are up on that stage. This is the best we can do since 'Cannibal' insists upon having the people see the bride paraded in front of them."

He tried to rationalize the perilous decision, but he didn't even convince himself as he said, "At least we will be inside the perimeter walls."

The rising roar from the crowd spilled over the high walls of the garden. The energy captured Jack's attention, momentarily, as he walked the grounds supervising his required deviations to the stage.

Before the workers neared completion, the shouts for, "More flowers, more flowers!" came from the royal florist who was frantically working with his team to adorn the new addition of the runway and make it seamless with the stage.

One would never be the wiser to the last-minute changes, as the Palace gardens were festooned with flowers, fragrance, lights, and ribbons all woven into an extravagant tapestry of delight for the royal wedding.

Just as the final touches were being completed, the guests were beginning to be ushered inside the perimeter wall, through the magical gardens, and shown to their seats. The orchestra's music played loudly, but it was being drowned out by the mounting chants of, "Behzar bebeeneem, behzar bebeeneem. Let us see! Let us see!" The outsiders, the uninvited, were pushing their way from the streets and alleys, attempting to breach the high walls of the gardens.

The entire security team had taken their watchful positions as Reza called out, over the radio, to all his guards, "You know what to do. Does everyone have clear sight?"

The vile one, Akbar, cut in to the radio communication, sheepishly purring, "Why yes, I've got a front row seat."

His snaggle-toothed grin could be seen by Reza, who was in position, a few yards back of Akbar's 'front row' seat. Annoyed that Akbar had gotten his hands on a radio set, he announced, "Let's keep the radio squawk down to the security team, *only*! No more banter. We're live; stay frosty!"

At center stage, Mahtab nudged her face between the thick, velvet curtains, that kept the secrets of the wedding ceremony wrapped in darkness. Her rosy cheeks and big brown eyes were all that poked through the folds of the lavish fabric. She was amazed by the size of the crowd. She ran back to Sadie, with the exhilaration of small child, announcing, "This is it, we are ready to go! You remember what to do? Your music, you know when... ok? To walk, ok?" Her English stumbled over her excitement.

As the late afternoon sun gave way to the early twilight, the sparks of light began their dance in the sky...it was time. It was time.

*Bong, bong, bong, bong.* The deep sounding chimes announced the official start of the ceremony. People began standing and clapping, bobbing their heads, and peering over each other in order to get a better view.

Behind the velvet curtains, the frazzled requests were being announced by a scrawny man directing each person to their designated spot. He called out to the wedding party and their aides, "Places everyone. Get in your places. The king is about to make his entrance."

The king made his way to center stage and self-righteously took his throne. Then Sadie was delivered to her position, standing next to him. Several assistants carried the train of her dress, and spread it out on display for the audience to view once the curtains were opened. They then quickly stepped off stage, as the last set of bongs sounded.

Sadie looked over to the king and nervously smiled at him; it was a reflex. He did not have the same reflex; only an arrogant 'let's-get-on-with-it-so-I-can-collect-my-riches' expression, donned his face. His existence was solidly and completely material, he was incapable of acknowledging the beauty, of the woman standing next to him, nor her sacrifice.

The orchestra began playing the introduction music as the curtains were drawn open, then the music played for Sadie to begin her walk along the runway, toward the waiting crowd. They roared as the bright lights exposed the royal couple for all to see, upon the stage.

Sadie viewed the throng; it was a lot to take in...more people than she had ever seen in one place and they were all focused in...on her. She took a deep breath, looked down at her feet, and wondered if they would fail her in this moment, as the pounding of her heart grew to a deafening crescendo between her thoughts. *I thought you would be ready for this by now...*

The music restarted, cueing her again, to begin her processional walk. Sadie began repeating the wedding planner's directions, to herself; *walk from the main stage, along the runway, wave, turn and return to the king, turn back around to the audience, and smile...* She repeated the thought, *walk from the main stage, along the runway, turn and return to the king, turn, and smile.*

She scanned the crowd again, stalling, looking for the strength to walk through the last of her duties that Jack had pledged on her behalf. The strength she sought was not to be found in the crowd.

Deep at the far end of the garden, in the shadow of the crescent moon, Jack leaned back against the perimeter wall. He lit a cigarette and took a long, satisfying drag, as he watched Sadie struggle in full view. Then he coaxed his plan along, under his breath, "Come on baby, take that step; let's seal the deal."

Off stage, far to the right, was Mahtab; tears in her eyes yet a reassuring smile on her face as the orchestra played the intro music *for a third time.* She gave Sadie a directional nod, as she quietly yet persistently persuaded, "Take the step my princess, walk for your people." Then, caught up in the moment, she called out impulsively, "You are the Light of our light, shine for the people!"

With that, Sadie put one step in front of the other. The crowd roared with excitement as they stood and moved closer to the stage and to Sadie, with each processional step she took. The cheering drowned out the music completely. Some sounded the loud "le-le-le-le-le-le-le" calls heard at Persian celebrations and others, came together with the harmony of their spirit, chanting for Sadie, "Attisheh ma. Attisheh ma." The now-familiar call became comforting once again, giving her the courage to walk the length of the runway.

With each step the crowd would get louder and move in closer. People were crying, and smiling and passing bouquets of flowers up toward Sadie; she didn't know what to do. Sadie looked back to Mahtab, who was gesturing to her to take the gifts offered by the people.

Sadie leaned over and received a few bouquets, took another step and she leaned in for many more, as she turned, she collected yet more flowers from the people that seemed to love her so. She walked back to her position, standing next to the king; Mahtab and two helpers ran on stage to relieve the armload of flowers.

The crowd cheered and applauded her every step of the way. It was a loud and celebratory sight to behold. Sadie was in awe of their adoration as the crowd undulated with energy and love; so much love! She felt it reverberate, deep within her being.

Suddenly, over the security radio, a guard shouted, "Gun! Gun! 9 o'clock!! Along the perimeter wall!! Guards rushed toward the assailant, while Reza and several others rushed for the stage.

Akbar was the closest, and fastest, as he jumped up on stage and made a leap to protect the royal bloodline.

*BANG, BANG, BANG, BANG, BANG ... ... ...BANG!!*

The radio blared out, "Shots fired!! Shots fired!!"

Sadie's body was lifted and pushed through the air as she fell to the stage with the weight of the world on top of her. Her head hit the stage, hard.

"They're down! Shots fired!! They're hit, they're hit!!" the radio screamed out with the voices of several guards at once.

Sadie tried to lift her head, but could not. She slowly turned her face toward the crowd as her cheek collapsed onto the floor of the stage. She felt a warm, sticky liquid begin to pool beneath her. She faintly opened her eyes and looked over all the distraught people, moving in slow motion, in and out of her tunnel of sight. Everyone was screaming, some running, some ducking; all she heard was a dull ringing. Her vision began to blur as she glanced over the distorted mass.

Almost unconscious, she smiled at the trick her mind was now playing, as she saw two men, of many, running to reach her.  Sadie called out to them, in her thoughts,

*Ali!..Jason!...I'm here.*  Then…

*Stillness.*

*Silence.*

*Darkness.*

Chapter Twenty

*Stillness...*

*Silence...*

*Light...*

*So much light. It is so bright, where am I?* Sadie was
dreamy in movement yet alert of mind. She felt herself in a
loving embrace; one like a newborn child, in the arms of a
mother, for the very first time.

She discovered words, silently, in her mind, *I am
floating...on wings of light.*

Love, introduced itself to her, as she felt a breeze caress
her face and place a soft kiss on her forehead. She welcomed
it. Her thoughts resonated toward the sensation as she
proclaimed, *I have never felt a Love like this before.*

*"Oh my beautiful girl, you've found your way to me."* Sadie internally sensed the voice of an angel. *"You are the Light of my Light."* The words, again, were understood, not heard, as Sadie confirmed, that the angelic tones were not recognized as her own voice.

Her intuition was informing her, as words found their way into her understanding, *This is all so beautiful, pure, and peaceful. It must be the voice of an angel;* she accepted the thought as truth.

Gently, Sadie was released from the embrace, to float in the ether. A brilliant angel with wings of light, appeared before her in a flowing white dress, made of luminescent rays. The angel emanated the purity of love; Sadie felt the energy deep within as the words became present to her being again, *Is this heaven? Are you my guardian angel? I want to stay here with you...forever. Can I stay here? With you?*

Sadie's desires reverberated from her thoughts, filling the heart of the angel. Then the angel conveyed, *"Maybe one day, but you will not choose to stay, not now."*

Sadie was confused, *You mean I CAN'T stay...here...with you?*

The angel wrapped Sadie in her wings again before she explained, *"No my dear child, you have free will, therefore, you will choose the right path for your journey."* With a ray of encouragement she continued, *"I have foreseen your potential, for it is written in the ether, and illuminated by the fire of the stars under which you were born."*

Sadie was at peace yet intently focused on every detail of what was being revealed to her.

The angel continued, *"Cassandra, my dearest one, you get to choose your next step; it will not be an easy decision, but greatness comes to those with courage. Use discernment, with all that you learn, past, present, and that which has yet to unfold. Use intuition, to help guide your way. Above all, seek Truth. Truth is the light which pierces darkness to reveal the Unknown. Let these be your guiding principles and they will guide each step along your journey.*" With those words, the angel set Sadie free, into the ether once again.

The light began to fade as Sadie felt herself faltering…failing…falling…down, down, down. Frantic, she called out aloud, "Wait! Wait, I am scared, I don't want to leave! I choose to stay, here with you! I am *choosing* to stay!" she demanded. "How will I find you? Come back! Who are you!?"

A dim shaft of light reappeared, allowing the angel to give way to the image of a beautiful woman.

Sadie watched in wonder as the woman stood directly in front of her, in silence. Sadie could not believe the likeness she shared with the stranger; the color of their hair, the shape of their eyes, even the curve of their full lips, it was remarkable. "Are you here for me? Do I know you? Who are you?" Sadie asked of the woman standing in front of her.

Without a spoken word, the woman slowly lifted the hem of her long, tattered, skirt. Sadie watched in wonder, seeking answers, as she followed the rising hemline with curiosity. The woman exposed her bare feet, where the remnants of bloodied handprints wrapped around her ankles. Then she lifted the skirt higher, revealing a long, thin, scar beginning from above her knee, along her inner thigh, all the way up to her upper thigh. About mid-way, the scar pierced through a mark--a birthmark--which they both shared.

Sadie shuddered at the sight, "You have my birthmark! Are you...me?" Her intuition scoffed at the notion, before Sadie, once again, fell into stillness, silence, darkness.

*"Darkness needs light to know itself. Be the Light. It is your destiny!"*

Chapter Twenty-One

"Be careful!  Careful, damn it!!" Akbar bellowed at the guards that were moving Sadie's limp body from the stage floor and placing her onto a makeshift stretcher.

Mahtab watched, shaking her head, 'no;' refusing to accept the sight of Sadie just lying there, lifeless.  She turned away, only to see the king's body directly in view.  His face was ashen and his eyes just stared into the past.  Once his body was lifted onto the stretcher, the gaping bullet wound, at his jugular, was exposed; his blood had spilled out in a pool between the royal couple.

Mahtab quickly looked back toward Sadie.  The guards were rolling her onto her side to tuck the train of the dress under her frail body; just enough to enable them to carry her, unfettered. Mahtab shrieked in horror at the sight of all the blood. The entire back of the beautiful, white, dress was now saturated in red. She began sobbing and beating her own chest, with her fist. She ran to Sadie's side, held her limp hand and begged God to not dim this precious Light.

The guards tried to separate the two women. Mahtab refused to let go. The guards were unyielding, as they pulled Mahtab off to the side before lifting Sadie's stretcher. Mahtab tried to follow them, but they stopped her, with a forceful admonishment, "Security only!" Off they went in an organized frenzy, carrying both victims, to the medic's quarters.

Over by the perimeter wall, the first security guard had seized the gunman. Breathless, he reported back to Reza, via the radio, "The shooter took his own life before we could reach him. He shot himself in the head. He's dressed like a local herdsman; we are talking with a few people that recognized him. We will interview them and get back to the security bunker as soon as we have gathered the info."

Most of the wedding guests had scattered quickly from the scene; a few others were being ushered out by waiters and other attendees. The ceremony was over. The chaos was about to begin.

The guards carrying the bodies of the king and Sadie swiftly arrived at the medic's quarters, across the hallway from the security bunker, where Reza was gathered with his team.

Akbar entered the security bunker, breathless from running over to assist. He turned to watch Sadie being moved onto the medic's examination table. He yelled to the medic, "I want an update right away!" Akbar was visibly shaken from the ordeal.

The medic scrambled; desperate to attend to both patients, but after a closer look at the king, he grabbed a large pair of scissors and called out, "Help me get this dress off so we can find the source of bleeding! And close those damn doors!!"

The doors to both the medical quarters and security bunkers slammed shut, almost simultaneously.

Reza dragged both his hands up and over his face and head; hoping to wipe away the reality of the last several minutes. He was well-seasoned, but the thought of losing a young life—this young life—made him sick to his stomach. Silently he said a prayer with an inaudible whisper at the end, "Attisheh ma, may your Light shine brightly again."

Reza looked up from his prayer and saw Akbar, nervously pacing in the middle of the room; which brought Reza back to his duty, as he began, "Akbar, you were the first to jump onto that stage; you lead the breakdown. Tell us everything you saw and heard from where you were standing. We will start from the targets and work in concentric circles out to the shooter."

Before Akbar could get a word out, the door flung open and in stormed Jack "Cannibal" Jones, yelling, belligerently. He did not slow his pace, as he lunged at Akbar, with one arm fully extended, the other ready to deliver his fist. His fingers wrapped tightly around Akbar's neck; his fury drove both men into the stone wall of the security bunker. Jack was seething with anger as he demanded, "What the fuck did you do?!! You screwed up my entire life with one wrong-ass move!!" He squeezed Akbar's neck tighter, choking off any possibility of a response.

Reza and the others jumped onto Jack. They separated the men and held Jack back.

Akbar was slow to move himself from where Jack had backed him into the corner. He rubbed the tendons of his neck, then slowly pulled out a chair, took a seat and watched, as Jack continued to unravel.

Jack's body was restrained by the guards, but his mouth was out of control, as he shouted, "How could you?!! You single-handedly destroyed a mission, twenty years in the making! What were you thinking?! Why the fuck didn't you save the *KING*??!"

Reza and the guards were taken aback at the words, but Akbar wasn't; he had come to know Jack quite well over the years of interactions. Akbar slowly leaned back into the seat of the chair, rocking it onto its two back legs. He looked at Jack, up and down, shook his head with disgust then tested Jack with his response, "Why didn't I save the king? Why Jack, I thought you would want me to save your daughter-- your own flesh and blood!"

Jack's eyes were bloodshot with anger; the veins in his neck and face were raging as he spewed out his venomous words, "Her!? She's the golden key to this kingdom... to this whole damn plan! A golden key I've had to carry around my neck like a frickin' baby albatross, for close to twenty damn years! 'Flesh and blood'?! Shit!! She's not my daughter! She's just an asset--a fetus in a basket I ripped from the hands of the haggard old bag I paid to kill her mother!!"

Reza and Akbar looked up at the same time. A blaring light, from of the examination room, was streaming through the reopened doors and into the security bunker.

In the doorway, where darkness battled the light, stood a naked silhouette, covered in dried blood, and wrapped in a medical blanket. Stunned and motionless;

Sadie…heard…it...all.

Chapter Twenty-Two

Jack's violent confession was heard by a few others, Miller, McCord, Woods, Stevens, Sanchez, and Ali, who had stepped into the room, behind Sadie; they were never far away.

Ali walked up to Jack, within inches of his face, and dispassionately commanded his men, "Cuff him."

Stevens was eager to oblige, "Yes, sir!"

Incredulous, Jack objected, "Cuff me!? Are you kidding, Ali? C'mon man, we're brothers, we go way back!"

Incensed, Ali retorted, "Brothers? You think we are brothers? Nah, you're not my brother; you're a disgrace…to me, to the uniform, and to the oath we took to serve and defend our country; you always were a disgrace, Jack! You think I hung around you because I liked you??" He grabbed

Jack by the collar and twirled his entire body, like a ragdoll,

in the direction where Sadie stood. "I was there for *her*! I

was there to protect Sadie…from YOU!!" Ali pulled Jack

close to his face, lifting him so they were eye to eye, as he

growled, "You weren't my brother; you were my *mission*!"

He shoved Jack, into a chair, hard. Then turned his back to

him. When he heard Jack wince at the pain of the cuffs

digging into his wrists he added, "You were always a pussy

when it came to pain."

Ali dropped his head and looked over his shoulder, back

toward Jack, "You're not too bright either, are you Jack? We

knew you were going rogue, even before you finalized this

mercenary plan twenty years ago, you son-of-a-bitch."

Ali came at Jack again, "We stand in the breach to protect

the innocent! How could you? How dare you? Take her

life…then take her child?" He did not wait for, nor want, an

answer from Jack, as he commanded his men, "Get him out

of my sight, before I kill him myself! Sticks, load him into the helo; tie him down good and tight. He's riding back to Fort Bragg with us; it's gonna be a bumpy ride!" Ali turned to Jack, "You know, the folks back at JAG are going to want to know, how you got so bruised and battered, before your official court martial, Jack."

Jack griped back, "What the hell are you talking about?"

Ali looked at Sadie, gave her a reassuring look, as if saying 'we got this' before turning back to Jack and matter-of-factly stating, "It's a long flight, Jack. A lot could happen."

Sadie was still standing close to the doorway, taking in every horrific detail, while staring at Jack with confusion and disgust in the same moment.

Ali walked back to her, took a hold of her hand, and gave it a long, hard squeeze, "You are not alone. We are here for you. We've always been near you Sadie; me, Jason, Akbar, you were never out of our sight." He wiped a tear that cut its way through the blood stains upon her cheek. "Hang in there, I know this is a lot. I promise you Sadie; you will be alright. You just had the wind knocked out of you…by that six-foot-seven, big lug, sitting over there. He was the first one to jump to your rescue." Ali nodded toward Akbar.

Sadie's stunned stare now fell upon the man she had always thought of as the 'Vile One.'

Akbar, gave a puckish look and shrugged his shoulders. "Guilty as charged," he confessed letting Sadie know that he too is part of the team, sworn to protect her. "I couldn't let Ali and his 'Special Forces' friends be the *only* ones having all the fun, now, could I? It is true, I have been working with Ali and his men, to protect you, from the *cannibal* we all know as Jack, and from the mercenary powers he aligned himself with."

Then, Akbar modestly stated, "It was the least I could do, after all I had put Miss Cassandra through."

She stood there, reliving glimpses of the shooting. *Akbar leaping onto the stage and pushing her up and out of the way...her body hitting the stage hard...being covered by Akbar as he wrapped himself around her, protecting her body with his own. Hearing each shot fired. Watching everything in slow motion, like a movie being shown, one frame at a time. She felt the comforting sensation of warmth seeping in through the back of her dress; only to come to the awful realization that she was lying in a pool of blood.*

Sadie looked away from her memory as her fears turned to rage. She scowled at Jack and lurched in his direction, not sure if she would strike him, or worse. Her skin was taught and stiff from being covered by the dried-on blood; feeling like a thousand daggers cutting into her flesh, making each step toward Jack incredibly painful...in more ways than one.

Sadie stopped herself; overwhelmed by the feeling of being lost in this darkness. She silently thought, *What am doing? I am all alone here, so completely alone...and lost...I've been in the depth of lies and darkness my entire life.*

She stilled her motions...and then her emotions, as she backed away from Jack. With each step, away from his evilness, the circle of darkness, secrecy, and loneliness, waned.

Then, she sensed a whisper, "The Light you seek...is seeking you!" She turned around, expecting to see her angel; it was her voice.

The whispered message pierced the shadows where Jack had kept the truth hidden from her for all these years. The truth grew into a fire within Sadie as she began to take back her stolen life, and step into her birthright, "I am no longer the little girl you kept under your thumb, inside the gates of that Virginia home."

The truth ignited the fire within Sadie, "You kept me in darkness, all my life. You left me alone, a lot. Do you know how many years I spent wondering why I was abandoned by my mother? And why *you* were abandoned by her? I have had such a deep desire to have just one memory of her…something to hold on to when I would wake up screaming in the middle of the night. But if I tried to get answers, or shed any light on my questions…What were your words to me Jack?" She screamed at him, "What were they!?" Then she replied for him, "Oh yes, the words are etched in my mind, as you would abruptly state, 'it is too painful for me, I don't want to talk about it, go to your room!' Too painful for *you,* Jack?!"

She again, felt the need to strike him; to unleash the pain she was feeling. Instead, she uttered, "You didn't even have one, single, picture of my mother; I should have seen through you, Jack. But your blanket of darkness is thick and heavy," she stopped to acknowledge her surrounding--held captive, in a bunker, in a palace, in Iran--before her light revealed more truth, "and your darkness reaches the far corners of the Earth."

Sadie took a deep, cleansing breath, then defined their relationship in one blow, "You are *nothing* to me."

She turned to walk away quickly, but the speed of truth being revealed was overwhelming. She fell backward into Jason's arms, fainting from the emotional battle that she had been forced to fight.

Ali nodded to Woods, "Help 'Sticks' carry her back to the tower suite. When she wakes up, let her know I will be there soon. We can all leave together, in the morning, instead."

## Chapter Twenty-Three

Sadie woke up several times during the night. The first time, to finally bath and cleanse away the bloody narrative of the past night. She then fell into a state of lucid dreams, where the cloud of darkness, that Jack had unleashed, encircled her again.

The nightmare became vivid as her thoughts battled between the light and the darkness, *I wish I could go back, back to that heavenly place and leave this life of lies behind. Take me, now. Dear God, take me away. What am I supposed to do? How can I move forward? Life was hard enough, growing up without a mother; not knowing who she was, or why she abandoned me. But now, what am I to do with all this? The man I had thought was my father—isn't.*

*His sickening confession, of having my mother killed and stealing me away at birth, is a burden greater than I wish to carry! Why am I here? Why was I even born into this world...For what? Money? Greed? Power?* Sadie tossed and tussled in her sleep amongst the jagged thoughts.

Meanwhile, Mahtab had snuck into her room just past the midnight hour, and sat vigil by Sadie's bedside; gingerly wiping the sweat from her brow with a cool cloth as she witnessed the torment expressed through her sleeping state. She prayed for her dear friend, then softly confessed, "I need you my dear princess. Your Light has been promised to us, to our land, and to our people. Freedom is forged by fire, and you are our fire...the Light of our light."

As Mahtab sent her prayers up to the sky, she looked up to see the moon's ever slow procession across the aperture of the tower window. She turned her gaze back to Sadie--the promise of Light--that yet, lay in slumber.

When Sadie began crying in her sleep, Mahtab hugged her and rocked her gently. Sadie awoke from the nightmare only to realize that the past night…hell…the past nineteen years of her life, were not only a bad dream, they were her reality. She confided, all that had transpired the night before, to Mahtab; letting the anger and hurt take turns expressing her pain.

Mahtab sat pensively and listened with her heart. Once Sadie had borne the entire, ugly, truth, and there was nothing else left within, Mahtab quietly whispered, "Darkness needs light to know itself."

The words unsettled Sadie, "Say that again," she asked.

"What? I just said, um, I said, 'Darkness needs light to know itself.' Why? Is that wrong? I should not say it that way?" Mahtab was unsure of her English, but not her belief.

"Those words, spoken just as you said it. 'Darkness needs light to know itself.' Those exact words were spoken to me, by…" Sadie looked into Mahtab's eyes, reaffirming their bond of trust, before she continued, "...by, an angel, that came to me!" She watched for a look of incredulity to appear on Mahtab's face, when it didn't, she continued. Sadie was drawn back into the memory of the angel, as she explained, "At the wedding, the shooting...when I blacked out, I went someplace...someplace heavenly. I was floating, in a vastness of light. In a realm where love is *known* not just felt. Love was not a mere passion between two; Love, just, was—It was All—It was One. I was in a state of being that was so full and beautiful and peaceful that words alone could never describe it."

Her memory then rushed back to the present, as she shared more with Mahtab, "But wait till you hear *this!* You will never believe me!" Sadie grabbed both of Mahtab's hands and held them close to her heart, capturing her friend's full attention as she began to elaborate, "The angel, she disappeared, and I became desperate for her to return...and...I called out for her, begging her to come back.

She didn't come. But then…this beam of light showed up, and in the light was this woman, not the angel, but maybe another angel, I don't know. It was super weird, because this woman, she… she looked just like me, by a lot. We could have been twins or something."

Sadie paused just long enough to inhale before she went on, "This woman, is just floating in the beam of light, she doesn't say anything; she's just standing there, right in front of me, then get this…she begins to lift up the hem of her skirt, and she shows me this gnarly scar, it's wicked long, but here's the part that shook me back to reality…she had my birthmark! On her leg!! The damn scar went right through it…*this exact mark!*" Sadie pulled aside the silk fabric of her robe to point to her birthmark on her right leg.

She stopped to look toward the bedside table where she had left the hand written note given to her by the elder at the bazaar. "Oh, oh, oh I almost forgot…the old man…the one from the bazaar! The guy that brought the ring back to me, remember him?" She ran over to the table and picked up the parchment he had used to wrap up the ring. "Look! Look at this symbol!" She pointed repeatedly at the gold-leaf drawing of a goblet of fire. "It's the same thing, my mark— it's my birthmark, he drew it, exactly as it is on my leg...how could he know? How is this possible?!"

She started pacing back and forth with a firm grip on the note. Then she chimed in again, "And he kept saying, 'It is your destiny!' over and over. I heard that same message, when I was blacked out! Seems like everyone knows my destiny, except me!"

Mahtab's eyes were shifting around, looking for answers; looking for a way to delicately approach what she was about to say. She peered into the tower room as daybreak was casting a pink hue into the entire space; inviting the women to join its gathering warmth.

Mahtab gestured to Sadie and said, "Follow me."

The two friends walked into the room, over by the circular rug, that lay beneath the aperture of the tower dome.

Mahtab asked of Sadie, "Do you trust?"

A hazy shaft of sunlight, from the rising morning orb, filtered through the window above.

"Trust? You? Of course, I trust you, Mahtab."

Mahtab asked again, this time pointing to Sadie's heart, "Do you trust, this? Your inner heart, your inner voice? Do you listen for it; do you trust, 'It'?"

Sadie's curiosity swelled, "Yes. I think so." Sadie took another moment then responded again, this time allowing her inner voice to express, "Yes, yes I do!"

The shaft of light increased its intensity upon the spot where they stood, as Mahtab began to slowly roll up the circular rug. With each pull and roll, a little more was uncovered. Once half the rug had been tugged and rolled away, it revealed a hole, in the floor, inlaid with a thick pane of glass.

Sadie's eyes widened and her mouth dropped open as she slowly moved closer to the glass window that had been built into the palace floor. "This has been here, the whole time? And we've just been walking over it??" She was almost afraid to peer into it as she leaned over and stretched out her neck to view what might be discovered. It wasn't until she had committed to step into the light that she saw it.

"Wow, that's amazing! But I don't understand, why is there a burning fire, under glass, under the floor of this room?"

Mahtab gave her a smile with the same warmth of love Sadie had felt from the angel. "Look again," Mahtab coaxed.

Sadie kneeled on the floor and took her time peering through the window in the floor. She saw the rubble of what might have been the walls of an ancient structure. In the center of the darkened space was placed a copper lamp. She examined the lamp closely, then half-frightened, half in awe, she exclaimed, "That's...that's my lamp; that goblet there,

that's my birthmark…what the hell?  Why is this here?"
Sadie throws her hands up to the heavens, "Help me, help me
understand all of this!"

The coincidences were too many and too quick to be
ignored as she rattled them off, "An old man with a note, a
beam of light with a woman that could be my twin, and now
a burning lamp of fire, buried in the palace floor, halfway
around the world, all have this lamp…this goblet thingy…my
birthmark!  It's not like it's some random tattoo you would
find on the arm of ten sailors in a bar during Fleet
Week…it's a *birth* mark, shaped like a flaming bowl!
Mahtab, what is happening?"

Just then, there was movement seen beneath the window
where she was kneeling.  A figure, dressed in white, with
their face covered came into view.  This person carefully
added wood to the fire of the copper bowl; the flame rose,
seemingly appreciating the veneration.

Mahtab kneeled alongside Sadie. She sought courage through her own inner voice, as it whispered, *Mahtab, you are named after the Moon for a reason--the great reflector of the light of the sun--the reflection of truth. It is time to reflect all that you know to be true.*

Mahtab began by answering Sadie's silent wonder, "He is a Zoroastrian priest. He adds wood to a fire that has burned for centuries inside the temple, the temple of our wisest ones, the Magi. The rubble and stones you see under this glass, are from the temple grounds, upon which this palace now sits. The fire, our fire! It is sacred to one of the world's oldest religions; its sacred to us."

A sweet scent wafted into their space as Sadie took in a whiff, "That smell, it would permeate into my room from time to time. I always wondered from where it came. The aroma always seemed to bring a sense of calm with it. I can't tell you how many nights that scent lulled my worries away and allowed me moments of peace during all this turmoil."

Mahtab explained, "The fragrant holy fire, which has been kept in that large, bronze goblet, has been burning for more than 1,500 years, consistently, in this temple, here in Yazd.

After another moment of silent prayer for the correct words, Mahtab went on, "When the winds of the west came to our land, it brought with it a fast-changing, modern world, eager to extinguish the light of truth and bury our ancient ways. The people were persecuted, so we scattered into the desert and went underground; our numbers dwindled, but the wisdom did not."

Sadie was completely engaged, "Please tell me more, tell me everything."

"Everything?" Mahtab asked. Again, her inner voice guided her, with a silent nudge, *Everything, the time is now.*

Mahtab gathered her thoughts, then slowly let each one enter the light. "About 25 years ago, things changed again, getting much worse. We noticed a growth like a cancer come over our villages. This power made strangers--foreigners to our land--very wealthy, while they destroyed our villages and made us very poor, like slaves. This power was overbearing, so again, everyone ran and hid. Everyone but one brave soul."

Mahtab felt electricity enter the room as she delivered the message to Sadie, "This brave one, made certain that there was always a light within the temple. Even though this wicked power had damaged our temple, she saw to it that the eternal fire was burning from what was left of the holy house. She did this for all to see, so that the villagers would know that the fire of our people, our traditions, and the great wisdom can never be extinguished."

Mahtab lifted Sadie's chin and looked deep within her eyes as she clarified, "She was the last flame keeper...she was of the royal bloodline. She was the only one, until..." Mahtab became quiet; too scared to reveal more.

"Well don't stop now!" Sadie implored.

Fidgeting, Mahtab found the courage to continue, "This beautiful soul, the brave one, she…she was…her name was Sephira. She was pure and good and kind. She was the beacon of light, guiding us through the dark waters of life. My mother, would tell Reza and me, stories of her fearlessness. She was a warrior, fighting for the truth for each one of us. We all loved her, like our own mother.

"Loved? Why did you stop loving her? What happened to her?"

Mahtab became overwhelmed, she burst into tears, saying, "We did not stop. She was taken from us!"

The static electricity became charged in the air around them; filling the space with a powerful energy.

Sadie sensed it too, as the energy developed into that wonder-filled feeling of love she had experienced in those fleeting moments shared with her heavenly angel.

Electric waves came rushing through Sadie, moving her. She too, began to cry.

Mahtab's eyes widened, expressing exhilaration and immense love in the same moment as she spouted, "I feel her presence! She is here; Sephira is here with us now!"

Mahtab continued to cry, skipped sobbing, and moved directly into bawling when she impulsively blurted out, "Sephira is here, I tell you! Your mother, is here, now!"

The words struck Sadie as if she had been hit by bolt of lightning!

The beam of light, which had been shining from the aperture above, fractured into the vision of a million rays, as Sadie endured the emotional storm unleashed by the truth of those words.

Then, slowly, a gentle calm emerged and collected the scattered rays into One; focusing their individual expressions, into the divine brilliance of Light.

This fullness of Light settled the turbulence within Sadie too. She felt herself being drawn to it. The stillness, silence, and Love surrounded her once again. The state of Love was almost more than she could bear. Her heart swelled with a sense of belonging to something bigger than herself, something pure, peaceful, and beautiful...*oh so beautiful.*

Then, amongst the resplendence, she was visited, once again, by the image of the mystery woman from her angelic dreamlike state. But this time, the woman was even more beautiful, as she shone with the refulgence of the Light that Sadie was sensing.

Sadie stood in awe, motionless; letting every atom of her existence be introduced to the woman floating before her— her mother—the woman she imagined in her dreams of yesteryear. Sephira.

The vision of her mother, lifted Sadie from the depths of loneliness, where Jack had abandoned her. Her consciousness blurred the lines of time as the ideals of the future faded into the memories of the past. Sadie stood in the present, accepting the glimpse of truth that can only be found in the singularity of now.

But it was a fleeting moment. The lies of her childhood, and Jack's confessions of last night, once again, had thrown her into the abyss of darkness, where the path to her future lay in oblivion.

That loving feeling, quickly morphed into fear. Questions, welled up from the pit of Sadie's stomach, carrying anger, resentment, and hatred with them, as she began to question the image of her mother, "Why did you let this happen? Why did you leave me?" Sadie began wailing in anguish, "You should have found a way to be with me! You should have protected me! From him!!"

Sadie looked up at the vision of Sephira as if she was looking at the face of God and demanded, "Why was I ever born, if *this* was to be my destiny?!"

*** 

The silence was deafening.

## Chapter Twenty-Four

Sadie stormed into the bed chamber with Mahtab following close behind.

Mahtab pleaded, "Please my princess, you do not understand. Please give me a chance to explain. You have the royal birthmark. You are the next flame keeper. We have all been told of your coming home. You are the light of my people, the light we have waited for, we have prayed for you to be brought back to us. Miss Cassandra, you are the one and only, you are the child of the royal bloodline, please listen, my princess…"

Sadie stopped and turned in her tracks. Mahtab could feel Sadie's breath as she shouted, "Enough! Just stop with the 'my princess' shit. I've had enough! I've *done* enough!

My duties here were completed the moment they cuffed that retched bastard that caused all of this!"

Sadie sauntered around the bedroom, searching for her belongings, "I'm packing my stuff and getting the hell out of here, first thing in the morning!" She rifled through the racks of clothes that had been brought for her, over the last several months. "God dammit, there is nothing here that belongs to me. Everything belongs to the 'royal bloodline'…and before you start up again Mahtab, I swear, I'll lose it if I hear another word from you!"

Mahtab stopped herself from speaking. She stared at the woman before her, she then turned her gaze to the light of the fire burning from under the glass window in the floor. Mahtab bowed to 'Miss Jones' and walked backwards, out of the room, and out of her presence, without another spoken word.

Silence. Again.

## Chapter Twenty-Five

"She'll get over it." Sadie said, trying to convince herself.

Still talking to herself, but loud enough for listening ears. Sadie went on…and on, "I don't know what she expects. Like, I'm gonna stay here, and stoke a goblet of fire with wood, the rest of my life? I'm 19, I'm American, I'm going home." Sadie began pacing back and forth and going back to the racks and racks of clothes as she gets fired up again, "She assumes all those chants, and becoming my friend, and telling me about some woman that she thinks is my mother is going make me move here? Here!? In Iran!!? Me??! No way!…I'm going home!"

As she shoved the hangers of clothes to one side, she saw a balled-up, makeshift, satchel made from a black scarf, laying in the corner of the closet. Poking out of the satchel was the sleeve of the bright green dress in which Sadie had arrived, into this nightmare.

Grabbing the dress and shoes from between the scarf, she laid the items out, onto the bed, and said to herself, "Welp, I guess that's it. I'm packed. As soon as I put on this dress tomorrow morning and get my ass on that helicopter, it's 'adios' to this place!"

She threw herself on the bed, exhausted, but not sleepy.

That pesky silence was now her only companion, until sleep paid a short visit.

## Chapter Twenty-Six

The silence was broken by a thundering voice, "SO YOU WANT ANSWERS!?"

Sadie fought to see who was speaking as she wrestled herself awake.

She sat, at attention, at the end of the bed. It was morning, but the sun was behind the mountain, and darkness still filled the room.

Sadie tried to brush off the voice that had so rudely interrupted her sleep, "Aaaah, these damn nightmares!"

She shuffled into the bathroom and splashed some water on her face. She dried it with a towel; holding it over her face, for far too long. Finally, she set the towel down and looked into the mirror. She picked up the towel again and began cleaning the mirror. She wiped and wiped as if trying to wipe away the image she was seeing.

Looking into the reflection she asked out loud, "Why God? What is the point? Why did you bring me into this world, into *this* life?"

The image of Sephira entered Sadie's reflection. She wrapped herself around Sadie and expressed, "Cassandra, my dearest one, God created you, to see what you would show Him."

A warm breeze sealed the message with a kiss on Sadie's forehead. She inhaled the wisdom and the kiss, as if this one caress was the first breath of air she had received after having been held underwater her entire life. For the first time, ever, she felt like she was whole, as the image of Sephira and the reflection of Sadie, became One. "I love you."

## Chapter Twenty-Seven

As dawn finally broke, over the mountaintop, Cassandra awoke to whispers...

\*\*\*

*Darkness needs Light to know Itself*

*God created you, to see what you would show Him*

## Chapter Twenty-Eight

## Going Home

Ali entered Sadie's room, bright and early in the morning. He clapped his hands and rubbed them together, eager to move out, "Are you ready to go home? This whole nightmare will be over in less than twenty-four hours."

"Um, yeah. I mean, yes. Yes! I sure am." Sadie walked over to the service door Mahtab would use to enter her room. She opened it, hoping to find Mahtab waddling into the room with her warm, friendly smile. The corridor was empty.

Ali went on; excited for Sadie, "Sadie, I don't want you to worry about *anything*. I've already made arrangements with the base, we have housing ready for you. We can have you supplied with whatever you need. You can take your time, and think about what you might want to do, if you want to go to college...I got that for you, I don't want you to ever worry about money or your safety. You will always have a home and I will always be watching over you."

Sadie was taking it all in. "Um, thank you Ali. You've *always* been there for me. That all sounds great...really, great," she said, distracted all the while, as she looked back at the service door again. Nothing.

She slipped on her shoes, walked into the bathroom. The reflection of an American woman in a vibrant green dress with chestnut locks gave her an empty stare back.

She tamed her hair and tied the black scarf around her face and looked at the image again. A knowing smile graced the reflection as she approved of the mandated headdress for her last journey into the streets of Iran. "Ready to blow this joint?" She asked the reflection; it didn't respond.

There was knock on the door. Sadie ran out, hoping it was Mahtab, though she never knocked before.

Akbar poked his head in, "May I come in. I understand our great palace will soon be deprived of the brilliance of Miss Cassandra. I have come to bid her a fond farewell."

Sadie came out to greet Akbar, "I never properly thanked you. I don't even know where to start. Am I allowed to at least give you a hug?"

Akbar smiled, and shook his head, "It would still be ill-advised Miss Cassandra; but I receive your gratitude. It was not only my duty, but my sincere pleasure." He walked over to the half-rolled carpet, and the glass portal leading to the goblet of fire. "I see you found our little secret. My guess is Mahtab had a hand in this discovery, yes?"

Sadie nodded and laughed a little, "Yes." Then she wondered, "Do you know where she is? I've been waiting to see her before I leave, and now…now, it's too late. I must go. Will you tell her I said, 'good-bye'?"

Akbar bowed his head, "Of course, Miss Cassandra."

Sadie took one last look around the room, pausing at the service door…still nothing. She walked over to the bedside table to blow out the night lamp that had been burning, night and day next to her. "I should put the fire out in this lamp." She attempted to blow out the fire. The flame danced, but did not blow out.

When Sadie tried to extinguish it again, Akbar expressed, "The radiance of your flame cannot be diminished, my princess." He bowed to her again.

Jason interrupted their moment, "We're all loaded up sir. We've stowed the 'baggage' out of sight, as you recommended."

Ali smiled at the thought of how his men might have loaded the baggage once known as Jack into the helicopter, before he said, "Let's move out. Time to go home, Sadie."

Jason and Ali led the way out, to the helicopter pad, in the rear of the palace. The thump, thump, thump of the helicopter blades cutting the wind fell into rhythm with Sadie's heartbeat as they approached the steel bird.

Jason boarded and gave his hand to Sadie. She put one foot onto the helicopter, as one foot remained on the Persian soil. She looked into Jason's eyes, then at Ali and finally back at Akbar.

She backed away from helicopter. Ali and Jason tried to help pull her back in, until they came to the realization that she did not want to leave.

Sadie grabbed Jason and Ali's hands as she stated her intention, "This is my home now. I am choosing to stay, here, with the people that claim to know my family. It is my destiny."

Jason tried to convince her, "But Sadie, you're all set Stateside, Ali made sure of it! Come back with us, come on now. Let's go home."

Ali knew Cassandra well, any arguing with the look of determination she now displayed was simply futile. He gave

her a hug, "I am a plane ride away. If you need anything,
ever, you will be able to find me."

Jason watched Cassandra and Akbar walk back into the
palace through the closing door of the helo; then he stated
what he knew to be true, "The radiance of your light will
never diminish, my princess."

## Chapter Twenty-Nine

Akbar escorted Cassandra to the door of her tower suite. His eyes were full of tears, though not one dared to roll away in her presence. He bowed to Cassandra stating, "The radiance of your Light has never been brighter than at this moment." He opened the door for Cassandra as she entered her palace, for the first time, by her free will.

She walked slowly down the hallway wondering what the future could hold, but steadfast in her decision. As she walked closer to the tower, she heard tinkering coming from the center of the room.

There, at a small table, filled with a giant platter of the sweetest smelling fruit, was a place setting for two…and Mahtab. She sat quietly, trying not to smile, as she peeled a Persian cucumber and sliced a juicy plum.

Cassandra ran to her side, "Mahtab, how did you know? How did you know I would stay?"

Mahtab looked up and said, "I didn't. But I prayed." She began to cry, "I prayed for the Light of our land to come home, for our people to once again be guided by this Light, for each person to use the Light to discern the truth from illusion. I prayed that the Light be returned to us all."

Cassandra lifted Mahtab's vision, as the light of truth filled her own, and simply said, "My dearest friend, I don't know much, but this I know...

"The Light you seek, is within you."

## Epilogue

There exists a Living Light within each and every atom of creation. This is where Truth lives, in singularity. Where the Unknowable (Darkness), emanated Light (all visible creation) to know Itself (Truth).

"The Light You Seek…is seeking you!"

# About the Author

## KATY TACKES

I am an artist and author who creates to unite us all through messages of Love.

My creations, and the messages I receive, come through me—intuitively—while I am painting or writing. I rarely set out to create a particular piece; rather, I am called to express the specific message that is presented to me at the time, whether through paint or prose.

Please visit my art gallery: www.KatyTackesART.com
If you enjoyed the writing, please read my first novel,

### EACH TIME SHE WAKES

I hope you will find the work to be inspiring. May the messages they convey be a whisper for your soul.